I'M IN HEAVEN

by

Terry Ravenscroft

Published in 2011 by FeedARead Publishing

Copyright © Terry Ravenscroft, 2011

The book cover artwork is copyright to Tom Unwin

British Library C.I.P.

A CIP catalogue record for this title is available from the British Library.

About the author

The day after Terry Ravenscroft threw in his mundane factory job to become a television comedy scriptwriter he was involved in a car accident which left him unable to turn his head. Since then he has never looked back.

Before they took him away he wrote scripts for Les Dawson, The Two Ronnies, Morecambe and Wise, Alas Smith and Jones, Not the Nine O'Clock News, Dave Allen, Frankie Howerd, Ken Dodd, Roy Hudd, Hale and Pace, and quite a few others. He also wrote many episodes of the situation comedy Terry & June, and the award-winning BBC radio series Star Terk Two.

Born in New Mills, Derbyshire, in 1938, he still lives there with his wife Delma and his mistress Divine Bottom (in his dreams).

email terryrazz@gmail.com
facebook http://on.fb.me/ukZ78e
twitter http://bit.ly/t0mVyB

Also by Terry Ravenscroft

CAPTAIN'S DAY
JAMES BLOND - STOCKPORT IS TOO MUCH
INFLATABLE HUGH
FOOTBALL CRAZY
DEAR AIR 2000
DEAR COCA-COLA
LES DAWSON'S CISSIE AND ADA
STAIRLIFT TO HEAVEN
THE RAZZAMATAZZ FUN EBOOK
ZEPHYR ZODIAC

PART ONE

ON EARTH

CHAPTER ONE

"Have you moved your bowels today, Mr Smith?" the student nurse had asked me, the previous day.

"I haven't got any bowels left to move, love," I replied. "The surgeon moved the lot out when he operated on me."

I was reminded of the nurse's *faux pas* when the book I was reading, *The Campaign in the Western Desert*, told of a soldier whose entire bowels and a good bit more of him had been removed by a shell from a German field gun. Nasty, but at least it was quick; and without all the farting around I had to put up with before my bowels went up the hospital chimney.

I laid the book to one side. The pre-op sedative was beginning to take effect, doing its job of instilling in me the desired 'couldn't care less' attitude, a state of mind ideal for facing an operation but not for reading about the heroics of British soldiers in the Second World War.

I turned my attention hopefully to the TV in the corner. Hopefully because I had noticed, courtesy of the pre-med I'd been given before my previous operation, how much better the programmes were when viewed in a semi-drugged state. It had certainly improved *Strictly Come Dancing*. When I felt a bit better, if I ever did, it was my intention to write to the BBC suggesting they might consider providing free

1

sedation out of the licence money so they wouldn't have to try so hard to make decent programmes. Not that they do try very hard nowadays

Watching the television reminded me that I wouldn't be able to watch it when I really wanted to watch it; tonight when Manchester United was taking on Juventus in the European Champions League. The ward communal set could only receive terrestrial channels and the match was on Sky. Satellite broadcasts for the hospital's patients could be obtained on a personal TV, but only at the cost of an arm and leg, even to those patients who already had only an arm and a leg.

I shared the ward with eight other cancer patients. Large parts of the hospital are modern buildings. Of the parts that aren't most have been modernised. The cancer ward was not one of them, a throwback to the past. Nurse Evans told me the money had run out before they got round to it and they'd probably be modernising it next year. I shan't be seeing it.

It is a large room dating from the Victorian era, with a high corniced ceiling and inadequate small, high windows, in which the smell of disinfectant habitually loses its daily battle for supremacy with the twin enemies of overcooked cabbage and stale pee. The decor also features overcooked cabbage, the colour of the walls having been painted this same shade of washed-out green. The floor-covering is more or less the same colour, where it isn't stained brown from the rainwater that leaks in from the roof. One day when I was feeling especially sorry for myself I likened the ward to a giant tropical fish tank, the nursing staff in their assortment of coloured uniforms being the tropical fish, the patients the shit and grit in the bottom. Not the ideal place to die, or even to brush with death, if there is an ideal place to die; Old

2

Trafford or the bar of my local on a Friday night, would certainly be a much better option.

I had learned from conversations with the other patients that three of them, to a greater or lesser extent, had always believed in God. Mr Hussein, pancreas, believed in Allah, which I suppose amounts to the same thing if you overlook the fact that Allah is a lot less forgiving of his followers than the Christian version of the Almighty and consequently has a much longer list of things you can't do without getting the wrong side of him. The remaining three patients had started believing in God within seconds of being informed of their various cancers. This had only confirmed to me something I had always suspected; that nothing, be it the influence of religious parents, the guidance of Sunday School teachers, travelling evangelists, faith healers, the hearing of strange ethereal voices, the seeing of holy visions, a real tear in the eye of a plaster Madonna, whatever, could make a man start believing in God more, and with greater haste, than to be informed he had cancer. As one of my Second World War books had succinctly put it, there are no atheists in the trenches.

One of the three new Christians, Mr Greening, kidney, whose skin was almost the same colour as the walls, now read the bible constantly. Another, Mr Broadhurst, liver, now not only watched Songs of Praise every Sunday but joined in the singing and encouraged the other patients to do likewise. The third, Mr Fairbrother, liver and onions - actually just liver, but Mr Fairbrother, managing to hold on to his sense of humour even in his adversity, referred to his cancer of the liver as such 'for a giggle' - didn't display any outward signs of being a convert to the faith, but this was probably because by now he was too weak to hold a bible or sing along with Aled Jones of a Sunday evening.

They had been discussing heaven only yesterday. Mr Broadhurst, liver, started the conversation. "I wonder what it's like?" he speculated. "Heaven, I mean."

"Oh quite wonderful, I believe, quite wonderful," said Mr Meakin, stomach, one of the patients who had always believed in God.

Listening to their conversation I wondered why, if it was so wonderful, Mr Meakin was putting himself through painful sessions of radiotherapy every other day in his desire to stave off getting there for as long as possible; but I kept out of their fanciful musings, I wasn't looking for arguments, life is too short. Life *was* too short.

"Yes but what is it actually *like*?" persisted Mr Broadhurst.

"I think it's all like little white clouds," said Mr Fairbrother, although true to form he may have been joking. "I think you sit about on little white cotton wool clouds all day. Playing a harp maybe." He mimed playing a harp to add graphic credence to his theory.

"I hope you do a bit more than sit about on clouds all day," said Mr Greening. "I sit about all day as it is, I'm a fireman."

"You get to play cards though, don't you," said Mr Braithwaite, testicular and large intestine, a two-time loser, and another who had always believed. "Perhaps you'll be able to play cards."

I expected Mr Meakin to quash this notion immediately and wasn't disappointed. "He most certainly will not be able to play cards," he decreed, from atop his high horse. "Gambling is a sin in the eyes of the Lord; there will be no card playing when you're in heaven, you can take it from me. Or sex."

This prospect didn't please Mr Fairbrother one little bit. "No sex?" He frowned. "I don't think I want to go to heaven if I can't get the legover every now and then; I'm a man who likes his legover."

"You won't have the need of the legover, as you call it," said Mr Meakin, sniffily. "You will be in the state of nirvana."

"So you *will* be able to play cards after all, Mr Greening." Mr Gearing, throat, didn't speak very often as it made his larynx even more sore than it was already, but had obviously felt constrained to point out Mr Meakin's error.

"Why will he?" said Mr Broadhurst.

"Well they allow gambling there," said Mr Gearing, putting his larynx at risk again.

"Where?"

"The state of Nevada. That's where Las Vegas is, they've got slot machines and roulette and all sorts."

"And the legover," added Mr Broadhurst. "You can get the legover there too. They have these hostesses. Long-legged hostesses."

"I didn't say the state of Nevada I said the state of *nirvana*," said Mr Meakin, before the others could get too excited about their prospects of gambling and legover with long-legged hostesses once they'd arrived in heaven. "You will be at peace with yourself."

"Not if I'm not getting the legover I won't," said Mr Fairbrother. "It makes me bad-tempered, you can ask the wife."

"Neither will I be at peace if I'm just sat on a cloud playing a harp," added Mr Greening. "I don't like harps anyway, I'm an electric guitar man."

5

"As far as not being able to have sex, I don't think you're right there, Mr Meakin," said Mr Broadhurst, after a moment. "As I understand it Allah is the same as God, it's just the Muslims' name for God, and when Muslims go to heaven - well they call it paradise - they get to deflower seventy two virgins."

"Now that's what I call heaven, you can put me down for some of that," said Mr Fairbrother, rubbing his hands together in anticipation. "Pass me a turban and call me Abdul."

"I think that's only if you're a terrorist and you blow yourself up," said Mr Greening. He turned to Mr Hussein. "Isn't that right, Mr Hussein?"

Mr Hussein smiled politely and nodded, although whether it was in agreement or that he was acknowledging Mr Greening wasn't clear as he was listening to Meatloaf on his CD player. (He's in the next bed to me and plays it very loud. I don't mind because I quite like Meatloaf. If it was Coldplay I'd have strangled him by now.)

At that point the discussion ended when Nurse Jolley wheeled in the medication trolley, the grisly contents of which were enough to stop a disc jockey talking, never mind a cancer patient.

The exception to the rule of people starting to believe in God once they'd found out they were going to die was me of course. Norman Smith. Even though I now had only weeks to live I still didn't believe in heaven and a life beyond death. When I'd been informed I had cancer I was tempted to start believing, but only very briefly; deep down I'd known it was all so much nonsense and had dismissed it from my mind almost from the moment it crept in.

The only other time I had considered the possibility of

there being a God, apart from when I was very young and hadn't known any better, was when I was sixteen and still at school. The captain of the school football team, although an exceptionally talented footballer, was both ugly and thoroughly obnoxious; I had conjectured briefly that perhaps God had made him a good footballer to make up for his being so ugly and unpleasant. However there was another member of the team, equally talented and exceptionally good-looking who was as pleasant as they come, and that had convinced me otherwise.

Now, giving up on the television - Mr Broadhurst had used the remote to switch over to 'Loose Women' and all the sedation in the world couldn't make that bearable - I returned to *The Campaign in the Western Desert*. But I found it difficult to concentrate and in no time at all my mind drifted back five months to the time when the beginning of the end had started.

CHAPTER TWO

A week after the beginning of the end had started I answered
the front door to find two Jehovah's Witnesses hovering
there. They smiled at me with their funeral faces and asked
me if I had a little time to spare.

Until a few weeks ago I looked young for my age; now I
knew that I looked older than my fifty two years. The sight
of the Holy Joes, poised like two vultures eyeing a meaty
carcass, aged me at least another year. As if the view from
my front door wasn't already a depressing enough sight
without two of God's Messengers adding to it. The other
week the milkman had said that with my luck if I'd been a
pair of knickers I'd have been bought by Ann Widdecombe.
He wasn't exaggerating.

I cursed. Why oh why hadn't I looked through the
window before answering the door? I knew that Jehovah's
Witnesses had a nasty habit of descending on the estate on
Sundays and that Hugh Gaitskill Street, Harpurhey, with
more than its fair share of sinners and no-hopers, ripe targets
both, was one of their prime targets. My mind though, had
been on other things.

The taller of the Jehovah's Witnesses had a threatening
stack of Watchtower magazines in his hand. He offered me
one and asked if I wouldn't mind reading it when I could
spare a minute. I wondered if anyone in the world could be
so short of something to do as to spend a minute reading
such a load of old bollocks. You didn't even get to have a
pint with it; at least when you were more or less forced into

accepting a War Cry or Young Soldier from the Sally Army the chances were that you'd be having a pint.

Whenever the Jehovah's Witnesses trapped me I would always just stand there and let them talk themselves out. Very occasionally it got a bit too much for me and I put a bung in their flow.

"What about Hitler?"

"Hitler?"

"If there's a God, what about the holocaust? Why did he let Hitler do what he did to the Jews?"

"He was testing their faith." This was said with absolute conviction.

"Did they pass?"

"Pardon?"

"I mean some test that, gas ovens. If you weren't one of the fortunate ones who'd been executed and had their skin made into lampshades. No multiple choice there."

"Millions of Jews still pray at their synagogue on a regular basis."

"Millions more don't." The Barbara Castle council estate had one or two Jews resident in its mean streets and I was pretty sure that only birth, death or marriage with a free buffet and bar afterwards would tempt any of them into a synagogue.

The Jehovah's Witness smiled. "We must all celebrate the Lord our God in our own way."

They have an answer for everything.

Another time they'd been going on about the miracles performed by Jesus. Tiring of their twaddle I said, "I haven't actually tried, but I'm fairly confident I can't walk on water. Can you walk on water?"

The JW looked puzzled. "No. Well of course not."

"And Jesus was flesh and blood, a human being, just like the rest of us?"

"Oh indeed."

"So how come he could walk on water while the rest of us can't?"

He had looked at me as though I were a small schoolboy who had just asked the teacher a very stupid question. "Well because he's Jesus, of course."

Priceless.

The only other time I had taken the Jehovah's Witnesses to task was one day when they'd been banging on about the goodness of God and Mr Swindells from number 30 down the road staggered past. Poor Mr Swindells has suffered from Huntington's Chorea for years and by now could scarcely walk at all. I pointed at him. "Look at Mr Swindells there. If there's a God how could he allow people to suffer like that poor bugger has to suffer every day of his life?"

The elder of the Witnesses refreshed his happy miserable smile and said, "God moves in mysterious ways."

I was about to point out that Mr Swindells moved in a mysterious way too but before I could the younger of the pair chimed in. "God only allows people to suffer who he knows will be strong enough to cope with the suffering."

I shook my head, utterly defeated. How could you argue with logic like that? I thought to ask them if God couldn't perhaps have chosen something less vicious than Huntington's Chorea with which to test Mr Swindells's faith, a wart on his nose perhaps, a boil on his arse maybe, but decided against it. They'd have some pat answer, they always do, what would be the point?

If they had called on me a few weeks ago I would have given them the time of day. Unlike most people I wouldn't have offered them some pathetic excuse or told them I hadn't the time to bother with them and shut the door in their faces. I would have liked to, but I've never been able to bring myself to do that. Truth to tell I felt a bit sorry for them; it couldn't be much fun, tramping the streets trying to find customers to share their delusions with more likelihood of having a dog set on them than they had of success.

My Auntie Betty told me I was too soft with them. They had door-stepped me a few weeks ago when she'd called round with an apple pie she'd baked for me that had gone cold by the time I managed to get shot of them.

"You should do what Reg did," she advised me.

I would have loved to do what my Uncle Reg did, but you have to be a bit of an extrovert for that; not me at all.

After being door-stepped himself Uncle Reg had followed the Jehovah's Witnesses, found out where one of them lived and at half past eleven that night had knocked on his door and asked him if he wanted to become an atheist. The ploy hadn't been entirely successful as the Jehovah's Witness had invited him in for a cup of tea and tried to get him to join them, but he and Auntie Betty hadn't been bothered with them since. "I told him what he could do with his God. And his cup of tea" Uncle Reg said. "And in no uncertain terms." I knew what Uncle Reg's uncertain terms would be and 'stick', 'up' and 'arse' would be three of the words he'd employed.

I couldn't do that. So I just listened to them, or pretended to listen, took their Watchtower and bade them goodbye. But that was a week ago. And a week ago I didn't know I had cancer. This week I simply closed the door on them and left them standing there.

Cancer. I'd known it was bad news from the way the

hospital consultant oncologist Mr Matthews had sucked in his breath before speaking, always a portent of bad news. "I'm afraid it's not good news, Mr Smith."

I knew instinctively what was not good about the news even before he told me.

"Cancer, I'm afraid. Cancer of the bowel."

"I see." I hadn't seen at all, I felt as fit as a fiddle. Nor had I any reason to suspect cancer, the blood test I'd had a few weeks previously had been for cholesterol (which incidentally had been fine; but what's the use of having a good cholesterol count if you've got cancer?) "Is it bad?" I asked, hardly daring to.

The doctor nodded. "It's in the secondary stage. Terminal I'm afraid."

That's three times you've been afraid, I thought. You're not half as afraid as me. Shitting bricks isn't in it. I knew my next question, I'd heard it often enough from people in films or on television dramas who had been cast in the same circumstances, the question they dreaded asking, the one they had to ask, the one I had to ask now. I steeled myself. "How long have I got?"

"Less than a year."

Less than a year? What sort of answer was that? Next week is less than a year. Tomorrow is less than a year. Couldn't he be more precise? Apart from that, didn't you get six months? It was always six months you got. Except for the man in the joke whose doctor told him he had five months to live. "Five?" the man had complained bitterly. "Why only five? Everybody else gets six?" But this was no joke. Cancer! Christ I was no age.

"With treatment," Mr Matthews said, breaking into my thoughts.

"What?"

"Your....er, time. That's with treatment. An operation followed by a course of chemotherapy."

As soon as I left the hospital I bought a packet of cigarettes and smoked five of them one after the other. I'd stopped smoking in 1992, ironically in response to an advertising campaign warning smokers of the dangers of cancer, but even twenty years on I still fancied a cigarette occasionally, so why not now? It wasn't going to give me cancer, I'd already got it.

Written in stark black letters on a shiny white background the packet of cigarettes informed me that 'Smoking Kills'. In the tobacconist's shop I'd noticed the same uncompromising message written on every packet, and in such large letters that for a moment I thought it was the brand name; that there were no longer cigarettes called Marlborough and Lambert & Butler and Silk Cut, that all cigarettes were now called Smoking Kills. It came as something of a surprise as I hadn't looked directly at a cigarette packet for years, initially so that I wouldn't start pining for a packet, later because I'd finally stopped pining.

While I was enjoying the cigarettes, and I really did enjoy them, I asked the "Why me?" question over and over again. What had *I* done to deserve it? Norman Smith? Who had never done anyone any harm in his entire life. Not on purpose anyway, not knowingly. Why not somebody else, somebody more deserving of cancer? People who deserved to get cancer never seemed to get it. Well no one deserved to get it - I'd never wish it on anyone - but it wouldn't have been the worst thing in the world if Mugabe or one of the other dictators that Africa constantly throws up was to cop for it.

It wasn't as if I hadn't always looked after myself. While no one could ever accuse me of being a fitness fanatic I had faithfully eaten my five a day, walked regularly (not being able to afford a car for the last couple of years helped), and went over the safe alcohol limit only occasionally and less than most. And yet there were people I knew, people well into their seventies, who smoked like chimneys, drank like there was no tomorrow and the only time they ever saw a piece of fruit or vegetable other than a potato was if someone was eating it on the telly they were slumped in front of all day eating crisps and swigging Coke. There was a family over the road, the Stanways, four of them, eighty stones between them if they were an ounce, all of them on benefits but each without the benefit of a brain to tell them they were eating themselves into an early grave. That last thought had made me sit up - it wouldn't be as early as the grave I was now headed for in 'less than a year'.

When I arrived home from the hospital the first thing I did was ring Bob Hill, Plumber, and told him I wouldn't be starting work for him the following Monday morning.

Six months previously I'd seen an advert in the newspaper sits vac columns, *Become a Plumber. Earn a Thousand Pounds a Week!* I answered it, signed on for the course, worked hard at it and had passed the exam, easy-peasy. A friend of mine once said about the profession of Painter & Decorator that if you could piss you could paint and plumbing isn't all that much more difficult, largely a matter of common sense and the ability to drink lots of tea brewed by grateful housewives with leaks. I had high hopes for my new occupation, imagining that being a plumber would be just the ticket. Or if not the ticket certainly better than being a wages clerk, stuck in an office all day, or at

B&Q telling people that the thing they were looking for was at the bottom of aisle B or the top of aisle C or was out of stock and could possibly be coming in next Tuesday with any luck. Being a plumber would get me out of the house too, and into other people's houses, lots of houses, which would enable me to meet lots of different people. Maybe I would be lucky enough to meet an English Rose? One never knew.

Three weeks job searching later, just ten days ago, after nearly two years on the dole, I finally managed to get a job. I had *Become a Plumber*. However I wouldn't *Earn a Thousand Pounds a Week!* Not now. Well what would be the point of starting work when I was going to die? Bugger that for a game of soldiers; it was my own plumbing that needed sorting out, not somebody else's. But that wasn't possible according to the doctor, you couldn't simply take out the old ballcock and put in a new one, you couldn't do that with bowels.

I thought to ask Mr Matthews for a second opinion, wondered why I hadn't asked him for one in the first place. Anyone could make a mistake, it happens all the time, especially in hospitals. There'd been a case in the paper not long back where they'd sawn the wrong leg off somebody and if they couldn't tell the difference between a right leg and a left leg they could certainly misdiagnose cancer.

I phoned the hospital. Apparently Mr Matthews' opinion *was* a second opinion, the first opinion having been given by his registrar Dr Cooley. "We do not take the decision to tell a patient he has terminal cancer lightly, Mr Smith," the doctor said in a firm but not unkind manner. "There is no doubt about it, I'm afraid." Afraid again. Was there anything he wasn't afraid of? A benign pimple perhaps? "It's a benign pimple, I'm unafraid."

Suitably admonished, and not bothering to seek a third
opinion, I apologised for wasting the doctor's time and went
out and bought another packet of Smoking Kills. "Is there
any brand that kills quicker than the others?" I asked the girl
behind the cigarette counter at the Co-op. "Double tar
perhaps? Only I'd like to get it over with." She either didn't
hear me, likely, as she was still talking to the previous
customer about her holiday in Ibiza, or concluded that I was
some sort of nutter, because after sending the customer on
her way with the information that Ibiza was 'shit hot and she
couldn't wait to get back there and out of this fucking hole
thank fuck' she just passed the cigarettes over and asked me
if I had a loyalty card. Is it possible to be loyal to the Co-op?
The Co-op is the shop you go to when there's nowhere else
open or for something you'd forgotten when you went to
Tescos.

The following day I told Auntie Betty and Uncle Reg the
bad news.

I think the world of my Auntie Betty, my mother's sister,
and wish she'd been my mother. My mother had been a pain,
a half empty glass person long before the expression had
been coined. True, she had been a semi-invalid, but then so
were lots of people, and they didn't go about all day with a
face like a week in Wigan.

My mother was the most contrary woman I have ever
known, could ever imagine knowing, more contrary than
Mary, Mary. If it had been my mother who had done the
gardening at 12 Hugh Gaitskill Street it wouldn't have been
silver bells and cockle shells all in a row that she grew but
deadly night shade and hemlock or something equally
noxious.

One of the many memories I have of her perverseness was the time we'd gone to the seaside for a week's holiday, Bridlington as I remember, although it could have been Scarborough or Whitby or any of a number of North Yorkshire seaside resorts she dragged me to once a year, all of which she had said were "Very nice but I wouldn't go again". I'd seen a boat trip advertised for later that week. Ten miles up the coast and back in *The Good Ship Saucy Lee*, stopping off at an island for swimming and lunch. I'd really fancied it. I like swimming and I like lunch. I knew my mother would raise all sorts of objections if I told her I'd like to go on my own, leaving her to fend for herself for the day. I also knew that if I suggested we both go she'd find ten reasons not to - the boat would break down and we'd be stranded for hours on end; there'd be a storm and we'd be washed overboard; a sea monster would emerge from Davy Jones's locker and swallow us whole; it would be another *Poseidon Adventure* and that had made her poorly just watching it, and don't mention *Titanic*. With this in mind I contrived to walk her past the sign the following morning. Pointing it out I summoned up a suitably derisive look, curled my bottom lip and said, "Huh, I don't fancy the idea of that!" Five minutes later tickets had been booked for the following day, sailing at 10 prompt, no refunds, bring a pakamac and waterproof footwear.

At dinner in the boarding house that evening my mother refused to eat anything. "I'm going on a boat tomorrow, aren't I," she said, as though it was all the explanation necessary.

"So?"

"Well I'll be seasick if I've got food inside me."

"Now you're being silly."

"Don't call me silly, I'm your mother."

"Well you *are* being silly."

"I am not. It stands to reason a body will be seasick if she's got food inside her and the boat starts rolling about the way boats do."

I sighed, long-suffering. "We're sailing up the north Yorkshire coast, Mam, not shooting the rapids."

"Are you trying to tell me it won't roll about?"

"Well it's a boat, it's bound to roll about a bit, that's what boats do, it's part of the fun."

"There's nothing funny about being seasick, it's horrible. People never eat the night before they go on boats if they've got any sense."

I tried reasoning with her. "How do you think people who go on fourteen-day ocean-going cruises manage? *They* eat every night before going on a boat the following day. *And* every day. Breakfast, dinner and tea. If they took any notice of you they'd go the whole fourteen days without having anything to eat. They'd come off the boat starving to death. I mean the main attraction of an ocean cruise is that you can eat all day every day if you've a mind to. And a lot of people do. Some of them came off a stone heavier than they went on. If everyone thought the same as you hundreds of people at P&O would be out of a job."

"Well that isn't my lookout; and anyway what's it got to do with the post office?"

My argument didn't make a scrap of difference. I knew it wouldn't. She didn't have anything to eat that evening, nor did she have breakfast the following morning. When we arrived at the top of the gangplank she asked the man taking the tickets how long we'd be on the boat. He said six hours. She told me she was already starving hungry, she couldn't

go that long without food and went bac'
gangplank. Back on dry land she turned to me,
of the gangplank, and said she hoped I didn'
gadding off enjoying myself and leaving her
day. I told her I wouldn't be enjoying myself, I'd ...
something to eat the night before in addition to a big
breakfast so I'd probably be spewing my ring up every five
minutes. She called me a cheeky young bugger - I was forty-
six at the time - and told me to get off the boat this minute.

I did as she commanded, much as I would have loved to
stay on the boat and call in at the island for a swim and
lunch; I knew that life just wouldn't have been worth living
if I hadn't.

When my mother was alive I often wondered if life was
worth living.

Things didn't improve much after she died, three years
ago. What difference her passing away made to my future
life was effectively taken away from me less than six months
later when the firm I worked for as a wages clerk,
Hargreaves & Son, went to the wall, taking Hargreaves, Son,
me, and two hundred jam and preservatives workers with it.
A slogan I dreamt up without too much trouble, 'No jam
tomorrow'- I'm not bad at that sort of thing and once won a
holiday for two in Cornwall ("Very nice but not as nice as
Scarborough") - was chanted daily by the redundant workers
outside the factory gates, in a vain attempt to save their jobs.

Hargreaves and Son was an old-fashioned firm, steeped
in tradition, which was the main reason it had gone under.
One of the traditions it was steeped in was having an
antiquated wages system, which I found to my cost when I
tried to obtain a position as a wages clerk with some other
firm and quickly learned that my wage clerking skills had

taken over by a technology of which I knew nothing. What was a spreadsheet when it was at home? A computer at Hargreaves's was as rare as a poor dentist and lacking a computer of my own - when I needed the services of one, usually for Googling something, I used the one at the library - I'd never come across spreadsheets, nor any other modern aids to wage clerking for that matter.

It soon became clear to me that even if I'd had the necessary skills to get a job I would almost certainly not have been allowed to practice them, as at the age of fifty two I was deemed to be too old. This seemingly arbitrary restriction also applied when seeking jobs other than that of a wages clerk. Jobs were thin on the ground anyway. One week all the Job Centre had was a vacancy for a Father Christmas. "But it's only seasonal." the clerk said, which if nothing else made me smile. I didn't smile an hour later when I was turned down for the Santa Claus job because I wasn't fat enough.

"I could be a thin Santa," I argued. "Where does it say he has to be fat?"

"The Santa costume is for a fat Santa. It would hang on you, it wouldn't look right."

"I can fill it out. Stuff old clothes and things down it to fill it out."

"You can't fill your face out. You've got a thin face. And it isn't jolly; Santa's got a jolly face."

"It's not jolly because I can't get a bloody job."

An oasis in the desert of unemployment appeared to be B&Q, a company that has a reputation for finding employment for people of sixty years old or even older. I applied to them but failed to obtain a position, and came away with the distinct impression that the reason I'd been turned down was because I was too young. It dawned on me that I was trapped in an eight year limbo, from age fifty-two to sixty, from which there was no escape. Maybe a job as a limbo dancer? I was certainly low enough to be adept at it, even if only metaphorically.

Fortunately I have been blessed with an enquiring mind - when I was ten my mother, in the ungracious way she had of saying anything even slightly complimentary, told me that I 'wanted to know the ins and outs of a cat's arsehole' - but unfortunately I had never used it to enquire into the possibilities of adding to the three GCE certificates (Eng. Lang, Eng. Lit, History) I had obtained at school. Nor since leaving school had I sought any further qualification that might have helped me better myself. It wasn't that I lacked ambition, more that I couldn't see much point in being ambitious if I wasn't going to benefit from it; the effort just wasn't worth it, there'd always be the smothering presence of my mother to put the mockers on it. In the light of recent events I wished I'd had more ambition, but you are what you are, so I'd gone my own sweet way. Then, when I'd finally been unshackled, it was too late to do anything about it.

Following my redundancy it wasn't too long before my money started to run out. I'd been earning a decent wage at Hargreaves's, much more than the indecent money I was drawing in Job Shirkers Allowance (which is what my fellow drawers of the pittance down at the Job Centre called the state handout).

My savings were little, less than a thousand pounds. Although by no means a liver of the high life I'd always liked to spend what little spare money I had on enjoying myself. Therefore, and despite making every possible economy, I soon had to start going without things I'd previously taken for granted; a holiday once a year, an hour or two at the pub on Friday night, a weekly visit to the cinema, a very occasional meal at a decent restaurant, nothing too pricey. All had to go, to some extent, the holidays completely.

By far the worst cut-back forced on me was in the following of my beloved Manchester United. My mother and I had attended all their home games since I'd been in my early twenties. (She also accompanied me on all my other leisure activities, her semi-invalid status being semi enough for her to demand a lot of looking after by her son but not semi enough for her to allow him the opportunity to sow anything in the way of wild oats.) I was forced to give up my season ticket. After twenty seven years. It was still possible for me to watch Manchester United - when they were playing at Old Trafford tickets could always be obtained, at a price - I just didn't have the price.

I was just grateful that my abiding interest, the Second World War, didn't cost me anything. Library books were still free to borrow - I'd always made good use of Manchester's famed Central Library and spent many happy hours there over the years - and nowadays there was the internet too, also free at the library.

I'd been fascinated by the war ever since I was a boy. I've no idea why, it just came up one day in History between The Industrial Revolution and The Corn Laws - our history curriculum seemed to be based on wherever our history teacher Mr Newton opened the book that day - and I was hooked. Learning all about it came easily to me, certainly much easier than my schoolwork, battles and blitzkriegs being a more appealing subject to small boys than geography and sums.

I became especially interested in the events leading up to the war; the coming to power of Adolf Hitler, the rise of the Nazi Party, the Nuremberg Rallies, Lebensraum , the annexing of Austria and the invasion of Czechoslovakia and Poland. I couldn't have explained my obsession with Hitler. It was just there, something I had. Why do some people go train spotting or try to catch butterflies? Perhaps it was because Hitler and me we were total opposites; Norman Smith, the sort who wouldn't say boo to a goose, and the German fuehrer who wouldn't say boo to a goose step. Maybe it was the sheer, almost unbelievable evilness of it all, the terrible attraction that violence often has for decent people - for much the same reason that the people least likely to commit grisly murders are the ones who are most fascinated by grisly murders.

Mr Newton called me a morbid little bugger and my schoolmates, no less understanding and more interested in the adventures of Roy Rogers & Trigger and Flash Gordon than concentration camps and U-Boats, made fun of me and my unusual hobby. Even Piggy Higginbottom, who on one occasion, after the Moors Murders had been in the news again, had spent an entire weekend shallow grave spotting. I didn't mind them making fun of me, I enjoyed my hobby. Stuff them.

A very strange thing happened when I was fourteen. I actually met Hitler. I knew it couldn't be him, really, because he was long dead by then, shot by his own hand in his Berlin bunker as everybody knows, especially me, but even by people who couldn't give a shit about Hitler. But it was just as real. I was playing football in the park after school with a few of my mates, just shooting-in, and one of them sliced the ball into the wood behind the pile of coats goal. I was nearest so I went to get it. And there in the wood was Hitler. He'd been watching us. He was a lot older than the Hitler I'd seen in photographs and newsreels, about eighty I'd guess, and his hair was grey. His funny little Charlie Chaplin moustache was nearly all grey too, and his face was all wrinkly, but if it wasn't Hitler it was his spitting image. The sight of him stopped me dead in my tracks. At first he looked as surprised as I must have looked, as though he'd been found out doing something he shouldn't, but after a moment he smiled, reached out a bony old hand to touch me and said "Norman. Wie geht's?" It means 'How's it going' in German; I know that now but at the time I thought he was telling me my end had come. I nearly shit myself. I just turned and ran. When my mates saw me legging it out of the wood one of them shouted, "Where's the ball?" and I said "Fuck the ball, Hitler's in there watching us!" They just laughed at me and jeered and told me I was Hitler bloody mad and to get back in the wood and get the ball it would be dark in no time.

When my father died young and I was forced, at the age of twenty two, to take on the role of family breadwinner and carer to my mother, I like to think that I played the poor hand of cards fate had dealt me with good grace. It wasn't the life I would have chosen but it wasn't the end of the world, there was still plenty to live for. In addition to my interest in the Third Reich and Hitler I had my books - I was always an avid reader - and my films, the worlds of make believe that provided the entertainment and laughs I didn't get nowhere near enough of in the real world. And I had my music and my football. My television too, though increasingly less of the electronic tit as the years rolled by. (I can remember when 'Coronation Street' was something to look forward to, not something that made you give up the will to live.)

Besides, there was always somebody worse off than you were. I knew somebody worse off, a girl of eighteen on the next street who had both her invalid parents on her hands, as well as a younger sister and brother to look after. If ever I started to feel sorry for myself I recalled the story of the man who complained he hadn't got any shoes, until he met a man who hadn't got any feet. Remembering the story one day when my mother was being particularly irksome, I thought that although I wouldn't like to be without feet I wouldn't mind not having to look after her and limping a bit, but unfortunately this option wasn't open to me.

Like most young men I would have liked to have girlfriends, and eventually marry. With the burden of my mother there was no likelihood of that happening. She never actively discouraged me from seeking a girlfriend; she never said I shouldn't have a girl. She didn't have to. Veiled comments were more than enough. "We're all right, me and you, Norman. Just us two, soldiering on," was a favourite. Another was "I see him down the street has split up with his wife. Far too young to have got married in the first place if you ask me, nobody should get married till they're at least thirty-five." On hearing this I asked her if this stricture applied to women too, as if it did it only gave them about ten years to produce children before the menopause cut short their fertile years. She told me not to "talk dirty" in her house, there was enough of that sort of talk on the television thank you very much without me adding to it.

By the time I'd reached thirty-five my mother had amended her minimum age for a man considering marriage to forty. Then forty-five. Then fifty. I was forty-nine when she died so never made the qualifying age. It wouldn't have made any difference; she would have moved it to fifty before I reached it, with fifty-five waiting in the wings.

When she passed away, and with her passing the obstacle to any romantic ambitions I might have passing away with her, I was at last able to start looking for someone I could share the rest of my life with. For so long a man without a purpose in life I set about my task with gusto.

I was still only middle-aged, of independent if somewhat limited means, and although I would never have been picked out from a crowd as the good-looking one I was nevertheless quite presentable; I didn't have BO, I still had all my hair, most of my teeth, and a penis, hardly used, one careful owner.

It proved to be a more difficult task than I could ever have imagined.

Although always comfortable in the company of men I was less so when it came to women, and was doubly shy when it came to the business of acquiring a girlfriend. I just never knew what to say to them and invariably ended up saying nothing. I could never approach a girl and ask her out, the embarrassment if they turned me down would have been too much to bear. Whenever a girl took my eye my usual method was to smile at her in the hope it would encourage her to smile back and maybe speak to me. If she did I would try to take it from there. On rare occasions it worked, but unfortunately for every girl who returned my smile and followed it up with a friendly word there were a dozen who asked me who the hell I thought I was smiling at and was I looking for a slap?

I once heard a story, maybe just 'a story' but it sounds like the sort of thing that might be true, of a man whose sole pulling technique was to go up to the girl of his choice and simply say "Do you fancy a fuck?" The story went that he got knocked back a lot but also got a lot of fucks. Never in a million years would I have been able to ask a girl if she fancied a fuck and even if I'd been able to the first slap of rejection would have prevented me from ever asking another.

Therefore my girlfriends were few and far between. There might have been more of them if I hadn't been so particular, for I knew exactly the type of girl I wanted. The problem was that the sort I wanted didn't want me and the sort who wanted me I didn't want. My Auntie Betty, whose opinion I valued, said I was too particular, and I suppose I was. But I knew what I wanted and wasn't about to settle for anything less.

My heart's desire was for an English Rose. I admired the demure, understated beauty of the typical English Rose; her lissom figure, her pale complexion, her unfussy, simply styled hair, blonde or brunette, usually long but not necessarily so, always with waves, never straight, never curls. Although I would by no means turn down a blonde my preferred choice was a doe-eyed brunette. And preferably one with three names - I had noticed that for some reason or other that those possessing three names were the finest of all English Roses.

But despite all my efforts I had never been able to attract an English Rose.

It was not for the want of trying. I had even tried internet dating, the Last Chance Saloon of those seeking love and affection, a meeting place which thankfully doesn't recognise tongue-tied in the presence of the opposite sex; even a dumb man can be loquacious on the world wide web,

Harpo Marx would have pulled. But even this had not harvested an English Rose, although willing English thorns had been plentiful.

One of those thorns, Sue from Stockport, informed me that her friends had often told her she looked a lot like Helena Bonham Carter. I eagerly looked forward to our speedily arranged meeting - the famous star of stage and screen was my second favourite English Rose of all time. When I met up with Sue I concluded that her friends must have been very good friends indeed, or in dire need of the services of an optician, as she looked more like Jimmy Carter than Helena Bonham Carter. Nor was her lack of English Roseness helped by her soiled anorak and the Capstan Full Strength dangling from her lips.

Fortunately she had said she would be wearing a black hat with a feather in it, otherwise I'd have walked right past her. She was also wearing a black eye, which would have presented me with another clue to her identity had she mentioned it, but had perhaps considered that the black hat was sufficient means of identification. Or maybe she'd got the black eye after our date had already been arranged; she looked like the kind of woman who could attract a black eye without too much effort.

"Sue?" I said in disbelief.

"Yeh."

"I almost didn't recognise you."

"I'm wearin a black 'at wiv a fuckin fevver in it aren't I?"

"Yes. Sorry."

Unaware of the protocol of internet dating I didn't really know where to go next. Sue from Stockport did. "We'll go for a drink shall we?"

"If you like."

Sue liked so much that we were sat in a pub in two minutes flat with drinks in front of us.

I had never visualised an English Rose drinking pints of black and tan, nor picking her nose and saying "fuck" every few words, and my date with Sue from Stockport was as short as good manners permitted.

I also tried placing a small ad in the 'Encounters Dating' section of the Sunday Times. (Not a great reader of newspapers - far too many exaggerations and downright lies - I took the Sunday Mirror, and only then for the football, but felt that English Roses with three names were more likely to take the Times than the Mirror. Auntie Betty made the shrewd observation that women of the ilk of Denise van Outen would be more likely to read the Mirror, whilst women such as Janet Street Porter would be more likely to take the Times, and which one would I rather end up with? I would have preferred to end up with neither, especially Janet Street Porter, about whom I had once had a particularly bad nightmare - a saddle and stirrups were involved - but felt on balance that my reasoning in plumping for the Times was sound.)

Not wishing another Sue from Stockport I took great care in composing the advertisement. I toyed briefly with the idea of stipulating 'those with a black eye who pick their nose and say 'fuck' a lot need not apply'. However feeling that these words were too brutally frank, and probably inadmissible, and unable to come up with words that would convey the same message in a less candid manner, I decided against it. I also considered putting 'teetotaller preferred' as I didn't want to end up in a pub again with somebody who drank pints of black and tan, and would have done so if I hadn't been aware that Greta Scaachi likes the odd tipple,

29

and I certainly didn't want to discourage any woman who looked like Greta Scaachi from replying.

After much deliberation my advert read: 'Single man, 52, GSOH, likes eating out, the cinema, reading, walking, WLTM lady 35-45, must be the English Rose type, for friendship and possibly more.' Of the three English Roses who responded to my advert one must have been at least sixty, another was almost certainly a transvestite, and the third, although the possessor of a GSOH, looked like SHIT.

I tried one further advert, which produced one response, from a woman who had 'mistakenly become a lesbian and was looking for a way back', and then threw in the towel.

*

It broke Auntie Betty's heart when I told her I had cancer. She cried for ages, and went on forever about how unfair it was. Why hadn't God taken her instead? She was seventy six, she'd had her life, I was only just turned fifty. I didn't say anything when she mentioned God. That was her business, let her have her illusions. At least she didn't go around knocking on people's doors and telling them all about him and shoving pamphlets in their face.

When she'd finally finished crying Auntie Betty told me that I'd best put my affairs in order.

CHAPTER THREE

....Uncle Sid's funeral last week. All the mourners were sat there at the crem, saying things people say at funerals.

"He's going to a better place."

No he isn't, he's going into the oven then up the chimney. He'll only go to a better place if the wind's in the right direction and it blows him to The Bahamas. If it's in the wrong direction he could end up in a worse place, he could end up in Accrington or somewhere.

"Well at least he managed to hold on until his cold weather payment went into the bank."

"We haven't got to kneel have we, Doris? Because I'll never get up with my knees."

All Uncle Sid's grandchildren were there. Texting each other.

"This is *so* not me."

Cousin Annie was there, with her little boy.

"Mam, is he going to be buried or crucified?"

"I'll crucify you if you don't shut it you little bugger."

Uncle Sid's four sons carried his coffin down the aisle, tipped down at one corner and gently undulating because Cousin Dwayne is about a foot shorter than the other three and Cousin Shane has a club foot. The whole event was being tastefully videoed by Six Feet Under Videos.

"Can you take him back outside and carry him down the aisle again just one more time? Only there was an aeroplane in shot."

An aeroplane?

"That little boy's tearing pages out of the hymn books and making aeroplanes out of them; you'll need to keep him under control. Oh and bearers, is that as straight as you can get the coffin because the wreath's going to fall off again if you're not careful."

They set off back down the aisle to start again.

"Where are they taking him now? He won't know whether he's coming or going."

"He's going."

"Well tell them to get on with it, they'll have me missing *Countdown* if they don't get a move on."

That's my Auntie Hilda, six vowels, five consonants, no brain....

Click!

I switched off the DVD player. Peter Kay is my favourite comedian but not even his latest million-selling DVD *Apparently A Bungalow Isn't Good Enough For My Mother, Now She Wants A Bloody Mansion The Greedy Cow* could cheer me up.

I would like to have been Peter Kay. Or any successful stand-up comic come to that. I often used to think what a wonderful feeling it must be to be up there on stage making the whole audience laugh, to bathe in the warmth of the waves of laughter flowing over the footlights. A countrywide sell-out tour, culminating in week at the MEN Arena, Manchester. Bring it on.

After I'd been made redundant and it had quickly become evident that getting another job was going to be virtually impossible I'd thought briefly of trying to become a stand-up. Well why not? It wouldn't cost anything to try. I can be quite funny; I knew that, people were always telling me. The milkman thought I was a scream. But the milkman was selling me milk and a strawberry yoghurt every day, he wasn't what you might call an impartial observer, and even if he hadn't been selling me milk and yoghurt it's one thing making the milkman laugh with a joke about not being able to get an erection since I'd changed to sterilized milk, quite another getting up in front of an audience and making it laugh.

It wasn't the first time I'd toyed with the idea. The other times I'd done no more than that, just thought about it, daydreamed. But the thought of my mother's likely reaction to my dreams had always stopped me doing anything about it: "What do you want to be a comedian for? You're far too young; nobody should become a comedian until they're a hundred." So that's just Bruce Forsyth then. Or *Sir* Bruce Forsyth as he's recently become. Jesus Christ, talk about the bottom of the barrel being scraped; we've scraped right through the bottom of it and a yard into the ground beneath it.

This time it was different though. There was no mother to pour scorn on me. This time I hadn't got a job to go to keep me honest. This time I needed the money.

I wrote a routine around how a good many Muslim bridegrooms don't have a clue what their brides look like until after they've married them as they'd always worn the burka until then. I made plans to try it out on open-mike night at The Frog and Bucket or another of Manchester's comedy clubs. Would it be funny enough? Were fame and riches just around the corner? Never mind fame and riches, was a half decent living round the corner? *I* thought my jokes were funny but, as a wise man once observed, a joke isn't a joke until someone has laughed at it. When I'd rehearsed the routine in front of the mirror the cat hadn't shown much enthusiasm but it hadn't walked out, but would human beings be as tolerant as Whiskers?

I thought of trying it out on the milkman but there was the sale of milk and yoghurt influence to take into consideration so he wouldn't be much use. Nor would Uncle Reg and Auntie Betty; they would laugh anyway, Auntie Betty because she loves me and Uncle Reg because he'd laugh if his arse was on fire, so I still wouldn't know if I was being funny or just deluding myself.

In the end I never found out. I didn't even make it to The Frog and Bucket let alone appear on its stage. I set out, but even on the bus I knew I wouldn't be able to go through with it. I could see it coming a mile off; if no one laughed at my first joke I'd simply walk off the stage. And I couldn't take the risk that happening what with the humiliation it would bring with it. It was the same flaw in my make-up that prevented me asking a girl for a date. The embarrassment of failure. I'd been fooling myself when I said it wouldn't cost anything to try - the cost was injured pride if it didn't work out and it was a price I couldn't bring myself to pay.

At that period in my life, and much as I tried to occupy my mind with other things, death was never far from my thoughts. Everything that came into my head seemed to work its way round to it eventually. It was like Six Degrees of Separation, except that I usually only needed five. Me....Hugh Gaitskill Street....Manchester....Manchester Southern Cemetery....Death. Me....My garden....Flowers....A wreath....Death. When I was feeling particularly down it took only four. Me....Go for a walk....Fall down an open manhole, land on my head and fracture my skull....Death.

When I followed my Auntie Betty's advice and sat down with pen and paper to put my affairs in order the whole process only took about ten minutes. There were only three things on it and one of those was 'Cancel the milk'. There was even a question mark against that, as not knowing exactly when I was going to die I didn't know when I'd need to cancel it. 'I won't be needing any more milk after June the third but I might just manage to hang on a bit longer' wouldn't be good enough. The other two items were 'Make will leaving everything to Auntie Betty and Uncle Reg' and 'Find home for cat'.

I didn't have anything in the way of personal effects of any great value that my auntie and uncle would be interested in, just a few bits and pieces I'd give to one of the charity shops when the time came, and there was no property to leave, 12 Hugh Gaitskill Street is a council house. During the sale of the nation's stock of council rented property in the eighties my mother had been offered the two-up two-down house at a favourable price - the cost would have been recouped inside ten years by not having to pay rent - but she had turned the offer down on the grounds that she might die before the ten years were up. (On exactly the same grounds she never took advantage of any 'three for the price of two' offers, preferring to buy one item at a time 'to be on the safe side'. At a loose end one day I had guesstimated that over the course of thirty years this policy had cost her about fifty thousand pounds. When I told her this she said it was a pity I hadn't anything better to do.)

"It would be just like me to die the week after I'd bought it," she said, when I suggested buying the house. "And then where would I be?"

In that little wooden bungalow with no windows, Mother. "Well if you were dead it wouldn't matter would it."

"I'm not being buried in debt, I wouldn't be

35

comfortable."

I'll put a little mattress in with you and a duvet, maybe a hot water bottle. "You wouldn't be buried in debt, they'd likely let me take the mortgage over."

"Yes you'd like that, wouldn't you. So that's what all this is about. Well I'm not buying it and that's all about it."

Apart from Auntie Betty and Uncle Reg I hadn't told anyone else I was going to die. I hadn't even told Bob Hill, Plumber; when I told him I wouldn't be starting work for him after all I lied that I'd had a better offer. I'd considered telling my mates down at my local, The Grim Jogger, but in the end didn't as I knew they'd only start feeling sorry for me and I didn't want that. They'd find out soon enough, anyway. And the council would find out when I stopped paying the rent; they were the least of my worries.

After compiling the 'Putting my affairs in order' list I turned to 'Things I want to do before I die'. It wasn't something I had planned to do. It had been prompted when I'd been looking through the television listings to see if there was anything I could watch that evening, in the forlorn hope that the BBC or ITV might have managed to coax enough life back into one of the dead horses they were still flogging for it to make one final lurch down the racecourse. I hadn't held my breath. I wouldn't have bothered owning a TV set at all, with its indigestible diet of cookery programmes and reality shows and make-over shows, if it hadn't been for the news and the occasional decent film or documentary. But there wasn't even a film worth watching that evening, nothing that wasn't an animated cartoon, which I've never cared for, or an offering that didn't rely on CGI, cartoons for grown-ups who have never grown up, which I cared for even less.

Amongst the day's offerings, sandwiched between *Chef of Chefs* and *Just Desserts*, or maybe it was between *Changing Partners* and *Granddad Swap*, was *The Bucket Men*, a film about two terminally ill old men played by Jack Nicholson and Morgan Freeman. I didn't bother to watch it; I'd already seen it at the cinema, it was a four piss picture that kicked the bucket long before the old men did. (I have always subscribed to the Sam Goldwyn method of categorizing a film's worth, whereby a great film is one which you can't bear to leave to go to the lavatory for a pee in case you miss something; good films were one piss pictures, not bad films were two piss pictures, and so on.)

The old men's list had been much longer than mine, whose list was not much longer than my list of affairs to be put in order. I nearly didn't make it at all. I didn't see a lot of point. To my way of thinking ninety per cent of the pleasure of doing something is in the memories of having done it; having memories necessitates having a future and I hadn't got a future now. I only compiled it to try to take my mind off things.

At one time my list might have been a lot longer, but only because it would have comprised of things I'd long since forgotten about, probably when I realised there was little chance of my ever doing them, what with my mother.

Making a list of things I *didn't* want to do would have been far easier. Being a member of the studio audience at a recording of *Strictly Come Dancing* or *The X-Factor* would be at the top of it; closely followed in joint second place by watching a *Carry On* film and listening to rap music.

There wouldn't have been a problem when I was a boy. The list would have been as long as my arm. It was a game I often used to play with Piggy Higginbottom, except that it wasn't 'I want to' it was 'I'm going to'.

"I'm going to walk on the Moon like Neil Armstrong."

"I'm going to go to Hollywood and meet Roy Rogers."

"I'm going to meet Trigger."

"I'm going to go up in a hot air balloon."

"I'm going to have fish and chips for me tea every day."

"I'm going to play football for England"

"I'm going to play cricket for England."

"I'm going to ride on a camel."

"I'm going to feel a girl's bare breasts."

I'd already felt a girl's breasts through her overcoat and jumper and it had been wonderful so what must feeling bare breasts be like? I could only imagine, and often did. Which led to, through the surprising but welcome arrival of an erection one day, another 'I want to'; 'I want to shag somebody'.

Less than ten years later most of my young boy's dreams had disappeared. Time, circumstances and my mother had seen to that. At twenty I had felt several girls' bare breasts - the first time was a one-night stand under Blackpool central pier with a girl from Ramsbottom who said she worked in a greengrocers. Which had surprised me because from the smell of her I'd have thought she worked in a fishmongers. (I know better now.) She was a junior swimming champion, a girl with big shoulders and a big nose along with her big breasts - this was before I had developed a taste for English Roses - and yes, it was even better than wonderful, it was bloody marvellous.

Riding a camel had been achieved too; I'd done that at Skegness when I'd gone on the *Desert Experience*, two hundred yards up the beach and back on a 'Ship of the Desert all the way from Morocco'. The excursion had lived up to its promise of 'making me feel just like Lawrence of Arabia', although as far as I could remember Lawrence of Arabia's camel hadn't stopped for a shit on the way back.

Now, short of ideas, I had turned to my good friend the internet to see what was on other people's wish lists. Some of the things they wanted to do I wouldn't have minded doing but couldn't on the grounds of cost. The air fares alone to such places as Australia to 'Scuba dive in The Great Barrier Reef', to India to 'See the Taj Mahal' or to Brazil to 'To go wild in Rio at the Mardigras' would take far more money than I was able to put my hands on.

Others, although affordable, didn't appeal or were unobtainable. 'Spend a night alone in a haunted house'. No thank you. 'Make love on a train'. I had enough difficulty getting someone to make love to anywhere without narrowing the field to women who'd do it with me on the 16.40 to Oldham. 'Fart in a crowded place'. I'd already done that lots of times and couldn't imagine there was anyone who hadn't, with the possible exception of the Queen and Joanna Lumley.

A way round the problem of not having the money would have been to follow the example of Geoff Jenkinson, up the road. Geoff, on learning he had a terminal illness and only months to live, had taken out long-term loans with six different loan companies. In all he borrowed £120,000, and had paid back less than £5,000 when he popped his clogs. He spent the lot on having the time of his life while he still had a life in which to have it. His Saturday night parties were legend. I was lucky enough to be invited to a couple of them and at the first had been introduced to Crystal champagne, crack cocaine and a complimentary prostitute all in the first five minutes. I had taken advantage of the first two but, still intent on finding an English Rose, not the third.

After much soul searching I opted to follow the Geoff Jenkinson method of funding wish fulfilments but after writing down the contact details of a number of loan companies I searched my soul a bit more and crossed them all out. Much as I would have liked to have taken their money - and a stream of letters through my letter-box constantly invited me to fill my boots with generous amounts of it - I just couldn't bring myself to do it. It was stealing, and I'd never been able to steal, it wasn't right, no more than it would have been right to fly the coop and leave my mother to fend for herself when my father died.

I ended up with just four things on my list: take a holiday touring the West of Scotland - I'd once set off for Fort William with my mother in a Wallace Arnold coach but on the way she decided she didn't like Scottish people so we'd got off at Junction 35 on the M6 and gone to Morecambe instead (very nice but she wouldn't go again); see the Niagara Falls; watch all Manchester United's matches in the forthcoming season, home and away; and have dinner at Raymond Blanc's *Le Manoir aux Quatre Saisons*.

Sadly, although it was something I would dearly love to have done, I had to strike from my list 'Strangle Ant and Dec', which I'd initially included for a bit of fun but later had started to think seriously about it. Well why not? It would have been a service to the nation. I've never got Ant and Dec. What are they for? What do they do? They can't act, they can't sing, they can't dance and they're about as funny as a walk round the park with a nail in your shoe. All they're good at is being Ant and Dec, and Ant and Dec can't act, can't sing, etcetera. But tempting as ridding the world of them was, and it was, it was impractical; I mean what would

Dec be doing while I was busy squeezing the last drop of life out of Ant? Not standing about waiting his turn that's for sure. And although it would get rid of fifty per cent of them - Ant, as he's slightly the more irritating of the two - it just didn't seem fair to strangle one of them without the other. My sense of fair play manifesting itself again.

Before I could make a start on the list I had to come to a decision. Mr Matthews, the oncologist at the hospital, had given me the choice of surgery or chemotherapy or both. 'Both' would be best, and was his recommendation; however none of the treatments would cure my cancer, just slow it down. Cancer with added extras.

In considering which, if any, to opt for, I had looked up the side effects of chemotherapy, or 'chemo' as Mr Matthews called it, in what I suppose was an attempt to make it sound more user-friendly. Chemotherapy? Was he having a laugh?

Apparently there are a hundred and fifty seven such side effects; I counted them. Removing from the list *Vaginal Bleeding, Vaginal Dryness* and *Vaginal Infection*, which I didn't think I'd cop for, even with my luck, brought the total down to a hundred and fifty four.

I'd never heard of most of them. *Anaphylasix* and *Neutropenia* were two of the most unwelcome sounding, but none were things I would wish to put up with a moment longer than I had to. *Bone Pain, Blood Pressure, Bronchitis....Cataracts, Conjunctivitus, Cystisis....Deep Vein Thrombosis, Depression* - Christ, who wouldn't be depressed if you'd got that lot? - *Dehydration, Dyspepsia.*

Amongst the more attractive things I could look forward to were *Bladder Problems, Itching, Impotence, Nosebleeds, Dizziness, Diarrhoea* and *Farting.* (I noted that if I had opted for 'Farting in a public place' as one of the things I wanted to do before I died that it wouldn't now present a problem. Not that I had foreseen one; quite often my problem is stopping myself from farting in a public place.) Especially, I didn't fancy my hair and teeth falling out, which were apparently near certainties. The list also included *A Dry Mouth*. I already had a dry mouth simply from reading about it so that just left a hundred and fifty three to go.

I considered my position. Deciding whether to opt for just surgery, or surgery and chemotherapy, the choice was no better than Hobson's. The former would possibly extend my life a little, but I would still die, the latter might extend it a bit longer and I would still die - but at the cost of experiencing any or all of the side effects and, after my hair and teeth had fallen out, looking like Gollum out of *The Lord of the Rings* whilst I was having them. However life, as the saying goes, is sweet, and especially so if you haven't got a great deal of it left, so I bit the bullet, while I still had teeth left to bite it with, and opted for both.

CHAPTER FOUR

In the event I didn't do any of the things I wanted to do before I died, save for watching just one of Manchester United's games - which they lost to a side they should have buried, the 'it never rains but it pours' principal kicking in again.

The operation, performed just two weeks after my cancer had been diagnosed, followed almost immediately by the start of the chemotherapy treatment, had left me so drained of energy that I just couldn't be bothered to make the effort. The only other thing I attempted, before I became too ill to travel all but the shortest distances, was a meal at *Le Manoir aux Quatre Saisons.*

On taking a seat in the dining room of the two-Michelin starred restaurant I ordered one of famed chef Raymond Blanc's signature dishes. However no sooner had I sat down than I started to feel sick - the chemotherapy - and by the time the dish arrived fifteen minutes later I felt so sick that if I'd eaten it I would have been in great danger of putting my own signature on it in the shape of a Technicolor yawn. There had been nothing for it but to leave it untouched. I was just grateful that *Le Patron* himself wasn't there to see the apparent slight on one of his creations.

If my problem had just been that I felt sick all the time it might have been bearable, but the ever-present nausea, from getting up in the morning to going to bed at night, was just the tip of the iceberg. Now seemingly every bone in my body ached, every muscle likewise. I had abdominal pain one day, chest pain another day, rectum pain on another, and on some days an unholy trinity of all three at the same time. The only time I didn't have a bad headache was when I had an even worse headache. And I itched. All over. My genitals in particular itched. They still itched after I'd scratched them, but this might have been because I didn't scratch them with the same intensity as the other parts of my body, probably because in the back of my mind was the fear that they might fall of and I would develop a vagina, and along with it the reinstatement of another three possible side effects.

In the past I had heard many people remark that they 'felt like death warmed up'. I had said it myself, many times. We hadn't known what we were talking about. *Being subjected to chemotherapy is feeling like death warmed up.* More than warmed up: grilled, roasted, pan-fried, baked in the oven on regulo 8 or 220 degrees for an hour.

And all to what purpose? What was all the pain and suffering I was putting myself through in aid of? I was going to die anyway. In 'less than a year' it would be ashes to ashes dust to dust time and the way I was feeling it would be in less than a month not less than a year. What a bloody awful state to be in. What a way to live. What a way to die. I could have cried. I did cry a couple of times, when it all got too much for me.

I once read somewhere that knowing you are about to die concentrates the mind wonderfully - a man in the condemned cell about to be hanged was the example quoted - and I could certainly vouch for it. The trouble was that it concentrated my mind on my approaching death, and no matter how much I tried I couldn't get rid of it for more than a few minutes at a time.

In attempting to, I re-read all my favourite books; I've always been able to get completely immersed in a good book.

I have my Uncle Reg to thank for my taste in literature. Not for pointing me in any particular direction as to what to read, but by his habit of leaving the book he was currently reading lying around the house. I'd pick one up.

"Is this any good, Uncle Reg?"

"Well it's making me laugh."

"*Riotous Assembly*? It doesn't sound very funny."

"Well it is."

And it was. I discovered I liked books that gave me a laugh along with the story and any message they might contain. Besides, I was never all that keen on messages, they're usually just the author's prejudices dressed up in nicer clothes. The novels of British authors Tom Sharpe and David Lodge and Guy Bellamy were and still are my favourites, although Tom Sharpe should have done himself a favour and packed it in while he was at the top. I'd read all their books at least twice, often getting as much pleasure from them on subsequent readings as I had on the first.

Not now though. I just couldn't concentrate on the words, good as they were. *Wilt* wilted. *Nice Work* didn't work. *The Secret Lemonade Drinker* didn't give up any more secrets. Five minutes was about the maximum I was able to lose myself in the trials and tribulations of Henry Wilt or Vic Wilcox or Bobby Booth before being dragged back to the reality of my own trials and tribulations. What is a tribulation anyway, exactly? At one time I would have looked it up. Not now.

It was the same with my favourite films, *Raging Bull*, *One Flew over the Cuckoo's Nest*, *The Godfather* trilogy.

Films that had previously held me in thrall, no matter how many times I'd seen them before, now failed to grab my attention at all. Even the Russian roulette sequence in *The Deer Hunter* failed to grip me, and that had always made the hair on the back of my neck stand out. But I didn't have cancer when I'd seen it before. It's different when you have cancer. Everything is different when you have cancer. Robert de Niro is conning the Vietnamese hoodlum into putting three bullets in the chamber of the gun, thus giving him a better chance of killing the little yellow twat when he turns the gun on him. Who gives a shit?

Nor did music help. Although I was a just a child in the 1960's my favourite music was the songs of that 'swinging' era. It was always playing on Aunt Betty's *Dansette* whenever I went round to her house, which was often as she was always baking lovely scones. In addition to my taste for the butter-plastered raisin-rich scones I developed a taste for The Beatles, The Rolling Stones and The Kinks, a taste which has remained with me all my life. I still can't eat a scone without thinking of the music of the early sixties.

"What's 'a dedicated follower of fashion', Auntie Betty?"

"Somebody who likes all the latest clothes, love."

"What's 'nothing to get hung about'?"

"It means nothing to bother your head about, love"

"What's 'I can't get no girl reaction'?"

"Shuttup and get on with your scone."

Wonderful music. Auntie Betty used to say she was spoiled when it came to music and I agreed with her. Certainly there's been little to compare with it since. Maybe the music didn't die when Don Maclean sung that it had in *American Pie*, with the death of Buddy Holly, but since the coming of boy bands and girl bands and rap and hip-hop it's certainly on the critical list.

I like my music as much as I like anything, and as with all lovers of music can get completely lost in it. Not then though. Not when I had cancer. If anything listening to music was less successful than books and films in preventing my mind from drifting off to the graveyard.

One day Auntie Betty asked me what music I would like played at my funeral. She apologised in advance and said she didn't like to bring it up but if she didn't and it was left to the vicar he might play something I didn't like. It didn't have to be hymns, she said, people had all sorts of music played at their funeral nowadays, when it was her time to go she was having *Spirit in the Sky* and *The Old Rugged Cross* but she'd been to a funeral the other week where the woman had had the *Twenty-third Psalm* and *Another One Bites the Dust*. I told her they could play anything they'd a mind to, *Call out the Fire Brigade* by The Move if they wanted, unless they were cremating me, when it might be considered as being in bad taste, I wouldn't be hearing any of it would I?

I soon discovered that life took on a different meaning when you knew you were going to die. Before, when you were doing something, you didn't wonder how many more times you'd be doing it, much less when it would be the very last time you'd be doing it. But facing death I thought of nothing else: the last time I'd ever be taking the bus from Harpurhey into Manchester city centre; the last time I'd ever look up at the night sky and seek out *The Plough*; the last time I'd ever be put the kettle on to make myself a cup of tea - would it be the last cup of tea I would ever make or would I be doing it again in an hour or two? It would certainly be the last time I would be doing it one day not too far away.

A week into the chemotherapy my food started to taste of

metal. Another of the side effects. I recalled that Bob Foster at Hargreaves's, when he was undergoing chemotherapy, had said everything tasted of metal, that if you were having fish and chips you might just as well eat the knife and fork. He was right. Steak, chips, meat pies, fish, pineapple chunks, custard, rice pudding, everything tasted like metal. How could sausage and mash taste like iron? They're meat and potatoes. But they did, along with everything else. "An ice-cream, sir? Certainly, what flavour would you like? We have steel, lead, silver, gold, uranium - that last one will bring a glow to your cheeks, my word will it - pewter, copper, lead, or how about this new one, tin & aluminium ripple? You'll settle for a bronze? A bit heavy on the stomach for some but that's my favourite too. And would you like it coated in mercury sauce and dipped in iron filings?"

I was eating less too, for I had little appetite; the wonder was, with everything tasting of metal, that I was eating at all.

A benefit of having little appetite was that because I was eating less I wouldn't be getting constipation, another one of the hundred and fifty four side effects. Or so I thought. Not so, for despite eating hardly anything it now started taking me longer to get rid of what I'd eaten. A soft-boiled egg for breakfast took four minutes to boil, five minutes to eat and up to two hours sat on the lavatory to get rid of. And it still felt the same size and shape as an egg when it came out, and with a lot more difficulty than the hen had had discharging it. I actually squawked like a hen once, which at least brought a rare smile to my face.

I tried not eating at all, not a difficult thing to do when a bacon sandwich tastes like a sardine tin without the sardines, but even then it still felt like I had constipation.

I went to my GP to see if anything could be done about it.

Dr Khan was about as much use as a concrete condom, and about as sensitive. "You are just going to have to put up with it, Norman. It is always the same story with chemo."

Chemo again. Friendly again, like it was a mate. Chemo Harrison or Chemo Higgins. Get yourself on a course of it Dr Khan, you'll soon find out whether it's friendly or not.

Three weeks into the chemotherapy my hair started to fall out. Not uniformly, so it didn't look so bad, so it looked like my hair was perhaps thinning slightly, but in big lumps, so that what was left were just tufts, a tuft here a tuft there, like a leather pouffe losing its stuffing. I went to the barber's and asked him to cut the lot off.

"Cancer is it?" he said, eyeing what was left of my hair. My face must have told him he'd supposed right. "I've done a few who've been on the old chemo."

I wished once again that people would stop trying to make chemotherapy sound friendly. Now it was 'the old chemo', even friendlier. Through gritted teeth I was about to put my thoughts into words when the barber continued, "Two of them made a complete recovery. They still come in. Regular customers." He paused reflectively for a moment and said, "Can't claim it was the haircut that cured their cancer though."

"It won't cure mine," I said.

"You never know though." The barber was still lost in the notion of the curative powers of having a haircut. "I mean barbers used to be surgeons at one time. That's why we have the red and white pole; it signifies blood and flesh. Not that I ever cut anybody," he added quickly, anxious to protect his professional reputation and the possible loss of a customer.

I wish you'd cut the crap and just cut my hair, I thought, and conveyed this by scowling and pointing at my head.

The possible curer of cancer took the broad hint and asked me if I wanted a No 1 or a No 2. I didn't know the difference but having just got rid of a particularly bad spell of diarrhoea I didn't want to tempt providence by asking for a No 2 so chose the No 1 option.

When I got home I surveyed the result in the hall mirror. If I'd had a pit bull terrier or a bulldog by my side I'd have been a dead ringer for about ten per cent of the male residents of the Barbara Castle council estate. Perhaps I should get one? And matching studded leather chokers for myself and the dog, like I'd once seen one of the morons and his moronic dog wearing. And maybe a pair of big leather boots and one of those leather waistcoat things they wear, and a tartan shirt and a few tattoos? It would certainly make the Jehovah's Witnesses think twice before ringing my bell again if I answered the door to them like that. No, not worth it, the price of pedigree dogs, even if it meant scaring the Holy Joes off until Kingdom come. Maybe I could put the cat on a lead? That really would put the shits up them; they'd think I was going crazy. Sometimes, then, I thought I was going crazy.

The Jehovah's Witnesses called again a couple of weeks later. Caught me on the hop again. What is it with them? Can't they find something more interesting to do? Stand watching the traffic lights change or something? I thought to tell them I had cancer. It might stop them coming back. I dismissed the idea more or less immediately; if they knew I was dying they'd probably be round every day telling me God had a place reserved for me in the Kingdom of Heaven. So I told them I'd got something cooking on the hob, a tin and aluminium stew, I had to switch the gas off, stay right there, I'd be with them in a minute. But instead I went out of the back door and walked around for an hour, left them standing there, gave them a bit of their own back, they'd kept me hanging about on the doorstep bored rigid often enough.

A week after I'd had the No 1 haircut my eyebrows and eyelashes began to fall out. I couldn't bear to look at myself in the mirror, I looked like a snake or the mock turtle in Alice's Adventures in Wonderland. I almost cried again.

I stopped taking the chemotherapy then. Bollocks to it, I was going to die anyway, I'd prefer dying sooner rather than later looking like a giant anaconda. When I told Mr Matthews he said it was my decision and that he understood. He didn't. He'd have to be looking like a giant anaconda with constipation and its food tasting of metal and dying of cancer to understand.

About a week after I'd called a halt to the chemotherapy I began to feel a bit better. At first I thought that maybe the treatment had worked but even as I thought it I knew I was kidding myself, it couldn't have, I'd already been told it was terminal, doctors didn't say you were going to die if you weren't; they sometimes said you were going to live when you weren't, but that was either because they were crap doctors or just to give you hope, and there wasn't any hope for me.

My feeling a bit better was short lived. Two weeks later I felt as bad as I'd felt before. Worse. Then Mr Matthews said another operation might help.

CHAPTER FIVE

Now, minutes away from that operation, a yelp of pain from Mr Braithwaite brought me back to the present. Nurse Evans, who was changing Mr Braithwaite's dressing, let out a concerned cry of apology. It made me smile. Not because of Mr Braithwaite's discomfort but because it was the first time I had seen Nurse Evans that day, and Nurse Evans was an English Rose.

I looked at her with both pleasure and sadness as she went about her gory business. With her lissom figure and long brown hair she would have been perfect for me. In her late twenties she was quite lovely, with the look of Audrey Hepburn about her, although not perhaps quite as beautiful as Audrey Hepburn, maybe an Audrey Hep. But although she was very friendly towards me, more friendly than she was to the other patients I liked to think, I harboured no illusions. How could I? For one thing she knew I was terminal.

I was aware of course that it is far from unusual for women to marry men even though they are well aware that their bridegroom isn't going to last for much longer than the wedding ceremony. But that was when they were in love; and although it wouldn't have taken me long to fall in love with Nurse Evans, if I wasn't in love with her already, I was pretty sure she didn't feel the same way about me. My one hope was that she would somehow guess I was yearning for an English Rose and, aware that I had only weeks to live, might marry me out of pity. I certainly wouldn't be able to ask her, my shyness, even facing death, the constant stumbling block. I'd tried looking at her in the way I'd looked at girls in the past in the hope they would start talking to me but she'd asked me if I was feeling all right and did I want a pain killer so I hadn't bothered again.

Another patient in the ward, Mr Statham, lung, was at the moment being comforted by the hospital chaplain, the Reverend Ever (known throughout the hospital as the Reverend Ever amen). The clergyman dropped by the ward every day to bring comfort to the members of his captive congregation. The hospital chaplaincy was the Reverend Ever's first position, having arrived fresh from theological college only a month previously, possibly pausing only to pick up a new dog collar and a pious expression.

Having comforted all the believers he now made his way over to me, the smile on his face vying for space with self-righteousness. I groaned when I saw him coming. At least with Jehovah's Witnesses you could pretend you weren't in. He stopped at my bedside and looked down at me in the condescending manner of someone who thinks he knows better than you, and said brightly, "Good morning, Norman."

"Bugger off."

When the Reverend Ever first started visiting me I'd tried being polite in rejecting his attentions, then I'd tried being politely firm, then just firm. None of these ploys had worked so I'd decided on a more blunt approach. For all the difference it made I might just as well have invited him to sit down on the edge of the bed and make himself comfortable, which is what he proceeded to do.

"You don't really mean that, Norman," he said, crossing his legs and opening his bible with all the eagerness of a sex-starved housewife opening the latest Jilly Cooper.

"Yes I do," I said, repeated the invitation and added, "Why can't you just leave me alone?"

Water off a duck's back.

He regarded me for a moment as though trying to come to a difficult decision. Eventually he said, "You look very much to me like a man in need of a little comfort, Norman."

"You look very much like a man who doesn't know the meaning of the expression 'Bugger off', Reverend Ever."

Water cascaded effortlessly off the duck's back again. He said, "I'll try to cheer you up a little."

I sighed. "I'm dying, Vicar. The only thing that's going to cheer me up is to be not dying. Can you tell me I'm not dying?"

He was well aware of my situation. "Well...." he started, in an effort to placate me.

I broke in before he could come up with yet another of the potted platitudes he seemed to have a never-ending supply of. "Well, my arse. There's nothing you can do, I'm a goner, end of story, end of me."

He persisted. "There is always hope, Norman."

"Not according to the doctors there isn't."

"You must never give up. Take our Lord Jesus."

"What about him?"

"What would have happened if Jesus had given up?"

"Well for one thing they wouldn't have nailed him to a cross," I said, after a moment's thought. I imagined this cruel but nonetheless valid judgement might just finish off the Reverend Ever and send him on his way to pester the will to live out of someone else. It did precisely the opposite. His face lit up like a beacon. "He *wanted* to be nailed to the cross, Norman. Jesus *wanted* to die. He *wanted* to go to heaven, so that he could be resurrected, so that he could

54

show us the way. He died to save us all."

"Well he's not saving me, is he," I said. "I'm dying, aren't I."

"But only so you can go to another place. Only so you can rise to heaven. Think of it as just moving on. I thought I'd already explained that to you?"

"And I've already explained to you that I don't believe in all that God in heaven, life after death stuff; it's bollocks."

The Reverend Ever gave a knowing smile. "Oh there's a God all right, Norman. He speaks to me quite regularly."

"I wish I could speak to him, I'd have something to say to him, by Christ would I."

"But you can speak to him. Of course you can. I speak to him all the time."

"Oh yes? Well next time you speak to him ask him why he's made it so I have to shit in a bag. Ask him that. Then ask him why he's given me bowel cancer. And given cancer to all the other poor buggers in here. And while you're at it ask him why, if he's God, he does such ungodly things, ask him why some people have to die long before their time and why people are suddenly struck blind, deaf, dumb or lame and little kids get incurable diseases. And ask him about tsunamis, pandemics, famine, earthquakes and umpteen other natural and unnatural disasters that ruin the lives of perfectly innocent people. No, Reverend Ever, if there was a God he wouldn't allow things like that to happen. And don't tell me God moves in mysterious ways and he only lets people suffer who'll be able to put up with it because I've already had that shite from the Jehovah's Witnesses."

Far from my tirade putting him off the Reverend Ever's eyes burned even brighter. "It is all part of God's great plan, Norman. Your death will not be in vain, believe me."

I turned away from him. "Look, just leave it will you." I'd heard enough.

The Reverend Ever hadn't said enough. "You'll see, Norman. When you go to your reward in heaven."

What was the point? What on earth was the bloody point? Theatrically I allowed my chin to drop to my chest, shook my head at the futility of it all, uttered a deep sigh and turned to face the wall in a gesture of dismissal.

My dramatics were completely wasted on the Reverend Ever, who prattled on regardless. The only bit I caught was about my circumstances not being beyond hope as long as I drew breath and that Jesus had once visited a man on his deathbed, cured him and told him to take up his bed and walk. I considered telling the reverend that if he did the same today the authorities would be on to him like a flash for encouraging the theft of NHS property but thought better of it as it might have encouraged him to extend his visit.

While the Reverend Ever was quoting something from Corinthians Two, male orderlies two suddenly appeared at the side of my bed.

"Time to go down to the theatre, Norman," one of them said.

The Reverend Ever expressed surprise. "You are to have an operation, Norman?"

I nodded.

All now became clear to him. "That explains it," he said, nodding his head in what he must have imagined looked like an understanding manner but which made him look more like someone having an attack of St Vitus Dance. "You will have been sedated. I understand now why you're not quite your usual self, why you told me to bugger off."

"Right, Reverend Ever. It's made me placid. If I hadn't

been quite so placid I'd have told you to fuck off."

*

The next to last thing I remember of my time on Earth was being asked by the anaesthetist to count backwards from ten. I hadn't bothered; I knew I would lose consciousness within seconds whether I counted backwards or not. Been there, done that, got the operation scars.

The last thing I remembered, in common with all people who are about to undergo surgery I suspect, was to wonder whether I'd ever regain consciousness.

The treatment planned was an operation to cut away the latest of the spread of cancer, followed by more chemotherapy. Apparently a new drug, some new course of 'chemo' - there it was again, good old chemo - had been introduced, and in trials had been successful in fifteen per cent of cases, success being judged as up to another five years of useful life. Mr Matthews had told me that I owed it to myself to try it, and in a weak moment I'd allowed him to talk me into it. Although in truth I couldn't have cared less; I'd had just about enough of a world that never seemed to tire of kicking me in the teeth. No one was more aware than I was that I wasn't leaving very much behind. The country had shot its bolt years back. Auntie Betty claimed she'd had the best of it and she was right. She'd been in her twenties in the 60's when the country finally shook off the effects of the Second World War and started to swing. We'd even won the football World Cup. We couldn't win an egg cup now. By the time I was in my twenties it was 1980 and the country had swung itself into something completely different. Political correctness had taken root and the suffocating presence of Health and Safety had begun to take effect. By 2011 both PC and H&S were rife and I'd had more than my fill of both. Too many things were now unacceptable that used to be acceptable. I didn't really want to live in a country where kids weren't allowed to play conkers any more in case they hurt themselves; in a land where gingerbread men now had to be called ginger persons; in a place where merchant bankers paid themselves more in one annual bonus than a nurse earns in a lifetime, just for moving money around; in a world where you couldn't smoke inside a pub and couldn't drink outside it (a few weeks ago I thought I'd got round this by standing in the open doorway of The Grim Jogger enjoying a fag and a pint, one foot outside and one foot inside, but the landlord had told me to cut it out, 'to be on the safe side'); and, and without at all ever wanting to call anyone a nigger, in a nation where black people called themselves nigger all the time, nigger this, nigger that, but let a white man call a black man a nigger and his feet wouldn't touch. What was that all about? Obsessed by celebrity and choked by apathy the country had not only gone to the dogs, the dogs had gobbled it up and shat it out. A fair dollop of it directly on me. Well fuck it, they could have it.

*

Suddenly, there was a white light. It took me quite by surprise, I'd been through four operations in my lifetime and in all of them it was as though no sooner had I lost consciousness than I was awake again, no white lights, no nothing.

I'd heard of the phenomenon of people who had technically died for a very short time before coming back to life, in which they'd reported a white light and a tunnel. And dismissed it out of a hand. But there was a white light. Definitely. And a tunnel too.

That was it though. Just the soft white light illuminating the tunnel and a more brilliant white light at the end of it. There was no sense of well-being, no feeling of being removed from the world, no perception of the body from an outside position, no intense feeling of unconditional love, no being presented with knowledge of one's own life and the nature of the universe, nor any of the other fanciful things that people reported they experienced after 'death'. Just the white light and the tunnel and the brighter light at the end of it.

The feeling I had was what I imagined it would be like to be in a womb and slowly making the journey through the vaginal passage towards the bright light, just like a baby going through the process of childbirth. Which in a way it was.

Oddly, it gave me a feeling of *Déjà vu.*

PART TWO

IN HEAVEN

CHAPTER SIX

When I came round from the operation I was sitting on a wooden bench in Piccadilly Gardens, Manchester. I noticed that I was dressed in the loose shroud-type garment that patients wear when undergoing an operation. I blinked in surprise. *What was going on?* How could I have got here dressed like this? I thought back. I recalled that I was in hospital. In the little ante-room where they put you to sleep before you go into the operating theatre. I remembered the anaesthetist asking me to count to ten. Then I had this weird dream about being in a tunnel.

Still drowsy I rubbed my eyes, fully expecting that when I re-opened them Piccadilly Gardens would have disappeared and I'd be back in hospital, back on Ward 12 with Mr Broadhurst, liver, and the rest of them. But when I did I was still on the bench. I tried again, rubbing my eyes harder and longer, but the result was the same. I checked my surroundings again. It was Piccadilly Gardens all right, no mistaking it; there was the Piccadilly Plaza hotel, there was the bus station, down the road a Metrolink tram trundled by on its way to Bury.

It dawned on me that I must still be dreaming; I was still under the anaesthetic, having a dream whilst undergoing surgery, like I did the last time they operated on me when I dreamt I was being chased by a horde of delectable English

Roses and no matter how much I tried to let them catch me I only succeeded in running farther away from them. More of a nightmare than a dream really; waking up in Piccadilly Gardens dressed in just a shroud was far more preferable, believe me.

I pinched myself. I felt it. So it couldn't be a dream. But if it wasn't, if I really was in Piccadilly Gardens, how have I got here? I couldn't have sleepwalked all the way from the hospital, it was over two miles, through city streets. Had leaving patients in corridors due to a bed shortage moved up a level? Had one of the nursing staff dumped me here until I woke up? I wouldn't put it past them - only yesterday a down-and-out who'd collapsed in the street had been left outside in a wheelchair for want of a bed and only prompt action by a security man had stopped the bin men taking him.

Before I could think of another test of my consciousness - I was still far from convinced, despite pinching myself, that I wasn't dreaming - a tall man carrying a brief-case and a clipboard approached me. He was aged about thirty-five and dressed in casual but expensive-looking clothes. His long, thin, pleasant-looking face smiled down at me as he indicated the place on the bench beside me.

"Mind if I join you?"

I was still too wrapped up in wondering what on earth was going on to respond to him. He sat down next to me nevertheless.

"Allow me to introduce myself," he said. "I'm The Archangel Phil. Your mentor. I'll be meeting with you from time to time until you're nicely settled in." He opened a packet of cigarettes and offered me one. "I believe you indulge in these things?"

My mouth fell open. I looked from the man to the cigarette packet and back. He indicated the clipboard. "My information is correct? You do like a smoke?" He took a cigarette from the packet and pushed it into my hand.

My mouth opened and shut silently a couple of times. Words eventually came out. "Can you tell me what's going on here? Why am I in the middle of Piccadilly Gardens?"

"You aren't; you're in heaven."

"What?"

"Heaven."

I rolled my eyes. "Do I look like I've fallen off a flitting? This is Manchester. I know Piccadilly Gardens when I see it."

The man nodded. "Yes, we always start off new arrivals in familiar surroundings. But after that it's entirely up to you. Many people head for the continent or the Americas; California and Rio de Janeiro are popular; The Bahamas too. The Maldives, of course. Personally I prefer England's green and pleasant, especially when the sun shines as often as I want it to."

Alarm bells started to ring. Suspecting shenanigans I looked around me.

The man picked up on this. "It's not a hoax if that's what you're thinking. There are no hidden cameras. Jeremy Beadle isn't going to suddenly leap out at you with that inane grin and cackle of his." He produced a cigarette lighter and snapped it alight. "A light for your cigarette, Norman?"

I sat up. "How do you know my name?"

He referred to the clipboard. "Norman Smith, fifty two years of age, single, 12 Hugh Gaitskill Street, Harpurhey, Manchester?"

"Besides, Jeremy Beadle's dead."

"As are you, Norman." His tone was authoritative, matter-of fact.

Despite the lack of evidence of any cameras or sound booms I was still far from convinced it wasn't some sort of wind-up. I sneered and dismissed this bloke who claimed he was an archangel with a wave of my hand. "Get away with your bother."

"You were having an operation, correct?"

"Are you deaf as well as daft?"

"In an effort to cure your cancer," he continued, disregarding the slight. "You were in quite severe pain, I believe. Are you still in pain?"

"A lot." As though to confirm this I put a hand to my stomach. But there was no pain there now, nothing, not even discomfort. I pushed down on my diaphragm, gently at first, then quite firmly. Still no pain. I looked at the man in hope. "Was it a success? The operation?" I didn't give him chance to answer. "Well it must have been, otherwise...." I paused. "But....I mean how come I'm in Piccadilly Gardens?"

The man shook his head. "The operation failed. The reason you no longer feel any pain is because you died on the operating table and have risen to heaven."

I pushed on my diaphragm again, as hard as I could, trying to make the pain come back. Nothing. Then I realised something. "My colostomy bag! I haven't got a colostomy bag anymore."

"That's right; everyone starts with a clean slate in heaven." The man paused for a moment then added as an afterthought, "Unless of course you *want* to have a colostomy bag. However I haven't come across anyone yet who does."

I took a few moments to digest the revelations of the past

few minutes. Could it be true? What this man who claimed to be an archangel was saying? Heaven? It didn't look like heaven. Not the heaven of people's imagination with angels sitting on little white clouds playing harps, like Mr Fairbrother, liver and onions, had jokingly suggested it would be. It looked just like Manchester. I took in my surroundings yet again. My eyes again confirmed it was Manchester. And yet....there was something different about it, something out of kilter, something not quite right.

It took a moment or two before I realised what it was. The buildings. They were the same size and shape as before, mainly Victorian structures littered with a few late twentieth century tower blocks, mostly hotels. But they didn't look half so grimy as they usually did. It was as though they'd all been newly built. And yet it *was* Manchester.

Now something else occurred to me. Although it was a cold December day - I recalled seeing snow on the roof of one of the hospital buildings through the windows of the ward - it was a lovely sunny day now, more like July in a good English summer.

The man seemed to have read my thoughts. "I spruced it up a bit for you and got the sun to shine. It's Manchester in heaven."

"What?"

"There's a Manchester on earth, and a Manchester in heaven; and an earth in heaven of course. Have you ever heard of a parallel universe?" I nodded. "Well it's a bit like that."

I struggled to take it all in. "So there's a London, too?"

"Yes, just like on earth."

"And a France. And an Australia?"

"Of course."

I shook my head in wonder. "Jesus."

"A Jesus too. Dead and well in Jerusalem."

"What? No, I wasn't asking if...."

The man smiled again. "I know. Just a little joke. You like a joke I believe? Big fan of Peter Kay?" He indicated the clipboard. "It's all down here." He tapped the side of his nose with an index finger. "Word to the wise though. Try not to use 'Jesus' as an expression of surprise now that you're in heaven; our Lord Jesus isn't too keen on blasphemy, as you can well imagine. God neither. Do not take His name in vain and all that. Try 'Upon my soul'. Much more appropriate." The friendly warning delivered he folded his arms, sat back and returned to business. "So then Norman, what would you like to do today?"

"Do?"

He checked his watch. It was gold, expensive-looking, like his clothes. "It's quite early; you have the rest of the day in front of you."

Still more than a little doubtful about the whole business I wrinkled my nose and said, "What was your name again?"

"The Archangel Phil. But you must call me Phil, everybody does. And you will believe it, I can assure you. So then, what's your pleasure?"

Only because I couldn't think of a good reason why not I decided to go along with it for the time being. "You say I can do anything I want?"

"Apart from altering your physical appearance or becoming younger. You have to stay the same age you are when you arrive here."

I thought about it for a moment. "What day is it?"

"What day do you want it to be?"

"What?"

"It can be any day you wish."

"I can choose what day it is?"

"You're in heaven; you can do anything you please."

"Can it be Saturday?"

"Every day can be Saturday. Time is timeless in heaven."

"And I can do anything?"

"Apart from the things I've mentioned."

I didn't even have to think about it. Not if it was Saturday, which apparently it could be just because I wanted it to be. "I'd like to go and watch Manchester United at Old Trafford. It's still the week we play....?" I broke off. What was I *doing*? Had I lost it completely? "Oh this is bloody ridiculous," I said. "I'm having a dream. I'm having the weirdest dream anybody ever dreamed; I'll wake up in a minute."

The Archangel Phil bloke smiled his patient smile. "Not a dream, Norman." He re-crossed his legs, put the clipboard down and sat back. "You were about to say?"

I accepted the situation, mad as it sounded. Besides, what had I got to lose? So, climbing aboard the nutter's express again I said, "It's still the week I died is it? United are still playing Spurs?"

"They can be playing anyone you wish."

"Anyone?"

"You're in heaven."

It was getting better by the minute. "Can they be playing Liverpool?"

"They're playing Liverpool."

And better. I saw snag however. "It's always an early kick-off when we play Liverpool. To control the drinking. What time is it?"

The Archangel Phil shook his head. "You still haven't

quite grasped how things are, have you?"

"What?"

"It can be any time you want. It can be ten-o-clock in the morning or ten-o-clock in the evening, it can be any day from Sunday to Saturday, any day from Boxing Day to Pancake Tuesday, it can be Saturday every day of the week if you want it to be, it's entirely up to you." He added a word of warning. "Although if I were you I wouldn't do it too often or you'll very quickly become bored with it. The vast majority of people here stick to normal earth timekeeping sooner or later."

I took a moment to digest this and said: "Right. It's Saturday. And I'm going to watch United play Liverpool."

"Excellent."

"Let's just hope they win."

The Archangel Phil chuckled and shook his head again.

I looked askance. "They *will* win?"

"If you want them to."

"Really?"

"Really."

I chewed on this and said. "Can they win five-nil?"

"If that's what you want."

"I hate Liverpool. I'd be in heaven if we beat them five-nil."

"You *are* in heaven."

"Right."

Something occurred to me. I dwelled on it.

"Why the rueful smile?" said The Archangel Phil.

I shrugged. "I think I might owe one or two people an apology."

"I'm sorry?"

"Jehovah's Witnesses. The Reverend Ever. Especially the

67

Reverend Ever. I just didn't believe them. Well why would I?"

"About there being a God and heaven you mean?"

"Well it all sounds so far-fetched. I mean we come from apes, not Adam and Eve, everybody knows that, Charles Darwin proved that."

"True. But where in *The Origin of Species* did Darwin write that there wasn't a heaven? As was proven to him when he arrived here, should he have had any doubts."

"Charles Darwin is here?"

"Charles Darwin, Charles Dickens, Charles Bronson - killing people in the movies doesn't count - and everyone else named Charles; Charles Laughton, Charlie Chaplin, Charlie Chase. In fact everyone who ever died is in heaven. Except for the ones who have gone to the other place.. And those who have gone back of course."

"Gone back?"

"To earth. Reincarnated."

"So there's reincarnation as well?" Another surprise. Broughie, a drinking acquaintance of mine at The Grim Jogger, had once claimed that the reason he was over-sexed was because he had been a bull in a previous existence; no more a believer in reincarnation than I was in God I'd told him I didn't know about a bull but he could certainly talk bullshit. Was this Archangel Phil bloke talking bullshit too?

Apparently not, as he now confirmed. "Oh yes, there's reincarnation. I've been back three times. That's the limit, three, then you're found a permanent position in heaven. I was Richard the Third the second time."

I was impressed. "Go on?"

The archangel glanced at his watch and looked apologetic. "Look you're going to have to excuse me; I have someone else arriving in Albert Square in a few minutes. Traffic accident, took simply ages to die in the wreckage. They're *so* grateful."

"*I've* been back, haven't I," I said suddenly. "*I* was reincarnated."

"Just the once, yes, according to my information."

"That tunnel thing I went through. I remember going through it before."

"The Passageway to Paradise."

"Who was I? When I was here before?"

"A serf."

I pulled a face. The Archangel Phil spread his hands in a gesture of sympathy. "I'm afraid we can't all have been Richard the Third."

"Richard Todd would have done. Or Richard Burton. I could have put up with the hangovers. What was my name? When I was a serf?"

He checked on his clipboard. "Timothy. Timothy of Chapel-en-le Frith." He read to himself for a moment, before going on. "Apparently you didn't have too good a time of it. The Lord of the Manor had you beaten frequently and ducked in the village pond for being fat and lazy."

I might have guessed. I said, "Why am I not surprised."

The Archangel Phil raised an eyebrow. "Your last incarnation must have been an improvement on that, surely?"

"Not that you'd notice."

He placed a reassuring hand on my shoulder. "Yes well now you're in heaven things will be simply brilliant for you, I'm quite sure of that. And now I really must go."

"Yes. Right." I realised that I was still in my hospital gown and had nothing on my feet. "What about clothes? I can't go to the match dressed like this."

"No. Sorry, I was forgetting. You'll need to do a little shopping before you hit the Stretford End." He pointed to a large corner building about fifty yards away. "There's Primark over there, of course."

"Yes I know Primark."

"New arrivals sometimes go there to get kitted out. Masochists mostly. However most people get themselves down to King Street where the quality is far superior. Hugo Boss is very good." He indicated his trousers. "I got these slacks there. The sweater is from House of Fraser on Deansgate. If this is the sort of thing you go for? "

"Aren't you forgetting something?"

"Like?"

"Like money." I patted my sides, indicating the hospital gown's lack of pockets, let alone any money in them. "What am I supposed to use for money?"

"You won't need any. Everything's free."

"Free?"

"This is heaven."

"Heaven." As I repeated the word I nodded as if to convince myself. Instead I thought of another snag. "And where am I supposed to stay?" Before he could reply I provided the answer myself. "Our house I suppose."

"Well if that's what floats your boat. But Harpurhey?" The Archangel Phil wrinkled his nose in distaste. "Might I suggest...."

*

Two minutes later the Archangel Phil trotted off, having arranged to meet me in three days time, when he would answer any questions I might have after my having spent a little time in heaven. Following that we would go house

70

hunting, if that was all right with me. All right with me? Anything was all right with me with the prospect of watching Manchester United hammer Liverpool five-nil that afternoon.

CHAPTER SEVEN

Tentatively, my heart in my mouth, I licked my lips, took a deep breath and pushed gently on the door of the Midland Hotel's Room 242. It eased open a few inches. Through the gap I could see a thick, luxurious carpet and expensive-looking wallpaper. Against the wall a vase of red roses sat atop an antique casual table, walnut I thought, maybe rosewood, expensive anyway.

I hardly dared step inside. Could this wonderful, wonderful day continue? Could it really end how I wanted it to end, how The Archangel Phil had assured me it would end if that is what I wanted? If only.

But why wouldn't it? Everything else had come true so far. Everything I had told The Archangel Phil I would like to do I had done; it had all gone like clockwork. However this final thing I wanted to do was the stuff dreams are made of. Manchester United beating Liverpool five-nil wasn't. It was unlikely, after all Liverpool are a decent side, but by no means impossible.

Like all true Manchester United supporters I hate Liverpool with an intensity bordering on the pathological; a hate returned in full measure by the Liverpool fans. It's only in the last few years I've been able to bear watching United play them at all. Previously I'd never been able to put myself through the sheer torture of it; not so much because of the nail-biting gut-wrenching intensity of not knowing the outcome until the final whistle but in case Liverpool should for some unaccountable reason manage to fluke a win.

Just seven short hours ago I'd been sat in the Old Trafford stadium waiting for the game to the start.

*

Red. Black. White. The colours of my favourite football team. The most eye-catching of colour combinations. Chosen for that very reason by the Nazi Party for their flag. I have never once been able to take my seat in the stands without being reminded of the incongruity of it; the Nazis a representation of evil, Manchester United a representation of good. Well good if, like me, you're a United fan.

The atmosphere in the Theatre of Dreams shortly before kick-off was electric, the chants eclectic. Insults in song were being swapped by the rival fans. 'Sign on, sign on, 'cos you'll never get a job' to the tune of *You'll Never Walk Alone* from the United supporters, countered by an equally insulting song from the Liverpool faithful about Ryan Giggs's extra-marital activities.

The preliminaries over, the match kicked off, the songs temporarily put on hold, replaced by roars and groans and impassioned pleas of 'Foul', 'Penalty' and 'Offside" to the blind-as-a-bat match officials.

After a fairly even opening ten minutes there followed a breathtaking display by the Red Devils, a truly vintage performance with five great goals, Rooney (2), Hernandez, Nani, Valencia. I watched the victory from an excellent seat in the north stand, just behind the directors' box. Sir Bobby Charlton was in attendance, which added to my already immense pleasure as the United legend is my favourite Red of all time. At half time, in the executive suite, I had enjoyed a slice of an excellent game pie, a generous portion of apple tart & fresh cream and a glass of champagne, all free to me, although everyone else seemed to be paying. Add this to an emphatic victory against the hated enemy, what more could a United fan ask for?

*

Well for one thing this United fan could ask for his day to end in the manner in which he'd told The Archangel Phil he wanted it to end. It would be the perfect end to a perfect day. If it happened, that is - as a man who has learned from experience not to expect too much of life I was still far from convinced. All right, I'd entertained similar doubts when earlier in the day I'd walked into the King Street branch of Hugo Boss without so much as a penny to my name, and that had turned out all right, but this was something else.

It had mattered not one iota to the people at Hugo Boss that I was dressed in a hospital shroud and had nothing on my feet. The assistant hadn't batted an eyelid, hadn't seemed to even notice. He couldn't have been nicer or more attentive if I'd been royalty, exhibiting just the right degree of obsequiousness to make me feel important without being at all fawned on. Would sir like a coffee before he made his selection? Please, if it wasn't too much trouble. No trouble at all, sir. Would sir like a biscuit with it? Sir would. Sir had a biscuit. It was very nice, the coffee likewise, just as I preferred it. He then invited me to browse through the racks of sweaters, shirts, trousers, etcetera at my leisure, and had remained at a discreet distance whilst I was doing so, ready to offer assistance and advice only if required.

I had purchased, if that's the expression for a transaction where no money changed hands, a nice cashmere cardigan that took my eye - the quality of which I could only have dreamt of buying when I'd still been alive - a casual suede jacket and gabardine trousers of the same eminence, a silk shirt, socks and underwear. A nice pair of brown brogues,

which I judged would have cost at least a hundred pounds
had there been a price tag on them, had been obtained from
Jones Bootmakers, nearby. Although I had always liked nice
clothes, without ever longing for them - I've never been the
sort of person who longs for things, save for English Roses
and Manchester United victories - I was more than chuffed
with my new wardrobe and planned to call in at both shops
for more purchases the following day when I'd have a little
more time at my disposal. For the time being though, I made
my way to the Midland Hotel and booked a room for the
night.

When I'd brought up the subject of where I would live
The Archangel Phil told me I could live anywhere I wanted.
It was entirely up to me. Why didn't I have a good look
round before deciding? There was no hurry. I had an
eternity. Literally. If I intended to stay in the Manchester
area he could recommend the Cheshire villages of Alderley
Edge and Prestwich, which weren't too far away; or perhaps
nearby Wilmslow if I wanted to live in a more populated
area and that much nearer to Manchester. In the meantime
why didn't I stay the night at a top hotel, or two or three
nights, a week or more, forever if it suited?

I had once visited Alderley Edge, on a trip out one
Sunday afternoon with my mother, both to see the
picturesque village and to visit the famous Edge itself. The
millionaires' retreat being way beyond my means, I had
never contemplated living in Alderley Edge, but that
afternoon had briefly considered pushing my mother over
Alderley Edge. But now? Well now I would have to give the
proposition a serious coat of looking at.

When The Archangel Phil mentioned it I told him that
thanks all the same but it wasn't likely I'd be living there, it

was quite a way from town and I didn't have a car. A minute later I was visualising myself behind the wheel of a top of the range Mercedes or BMW, having been informed by my mentor that all I had to do in order to make the vision come true was to get myself down to the nearest Merc or Beamer dealership and pick one out. Or a Jag perhaps, if I was a patriotic gentleman? I planned to make it my first job tomorrow morning and as I am possibly the most unpatriotic person who ever lived it would be a Mercedes.

For the time being though there were other delights awaiting me, inside the Midland's Room 242, delights even more seductive than a shiny new top-of-the-range German motor car. I hoped.

With bated breath I pushed the door fully open.

When I had first put on my new clothes, which fitted me perfectly despite being off the peg - it's all in the cut, sir - I noticed how much more confident they seemed to make me feel, how much they made me feel better about myself, how there was now a spring in my step that hadn't been there before. I can't say I was surprised - I had often heard that good clothes can have this effect on how a man saw himself, felt about himself - I'd just never had the opportunity to prove it. But whatever self-belief my new outfit had given me drained away the moment I stepped inside the hotel room, bags of confidence being replaced by the bag of nerves state brought on by the enormity of what might be about to happen. The nerves now proceeded to turn my stomach over. The result was a loud tummy rumble, followed by an even louder belch. I put a hand to my mouth to arrest any more belches that might be on their way out and cursed under my breath. But it was only to be expected I suppose. I should never have eaten as much as I had at

Michael Caines *Abode*.

I had chosen the film star's restaurant for my post-match meal. I have always had expensive culinary tastes without ever having the wherewithal to satisfy them - a saffron and truffle man consigned to a world of turmeric and button mushrooms - and now, at last in a position to satisfy them, I had no intention of holding them in check for a moment longer.

I'd always had an itch to dine at *Abode* ever since I'd read a sparkling review in the Manchester Evening News. The restaurant had opened a few years ago with the usual blaze of publicity and had since become a top choice of diners for miles around. While it may be true that nine out of ten newly opened restaurants are destined for failure this was never going to be the case with an establishment to which the name of Michael Caine was attached. I suspect that his name alone brought in as many diners hoping to catch a glimpse of the famous film star as it did people who came just to dine, people being obsessed with celebrity the way they are nowadays.

I imagined that getting a table without making a booking would be well nigh impossible and had been pleasantly surprised when I'd just pitched up and the *maitre d'*, no less pleasant and attentive than the assistant at Hugo Boss, had without the slightest qualm immediately found me a nice table.

The experience of dining at *Abode* was even more satisfying than I'd imagined. The food was exceptional, fully living up to the restaurant's Michelin star.

I started with *Pan fried scallops, tomato, aubergine and tapenade vinaigrette*, and followed this with *Cumbrian sirloin of beef potato galette, parsley purée, smoked marrowbone croquette and sauce bordelaise.* For dessert I went for the *Hot chocolate fondant, white chocolate mousse with cherry and kirsch ice cream.* All washed down with a bottle of *1982 Chateau Beycheville, St Julien.* It was probably the combination of all four items, plus the game pie and apple tart & fresh cream I'd had earlier at the football match, that caused my stomach to start playing up, but I blamed it on the dessert, of which he I'd had two portions, being a martyr to cream (I've my Auntie Betty to blame for that). But this was a special day.

*

And it was about to get even more special. With any luck.

I waited for my stomach to settle and, hardly daring to breathe, I stepped inside. I looked around. The room was empty. My world collapsed. At a stroke eager anticipation was replaced with abject misery. I gave the deepest of sighs. I might have known it was all too good to be true; this is Norman Smith here.

I tried to console myself. It wasn't the end of the world. The football had been great, the meal had been superb, I'd got some nice new clothes, you couldn't win them all.

You could win them all. As I now found out. And the final win was the best win of them all. For now the bathroom door opened and an English Rose glided out. She was dressed in a long pearl-coloured satin negligee that clung lovingly to her curves. And she was truly beautiful, much, much more beautiful in the flesh than her photographs or image on the silver screen, more beautiful than I had thought possible.

When The Archangel Phil had asked me how I wanted to round off my evening I'd had no doubts at all. A no brainer as they say. It was to spend the night with the epitome of

English Roses. And now here she was, standing in front of me, close enough for me to touch, smiling at me demurely.

"Hello, Norman," she said in that velvet growl she uses when at her most seductive.

She made her way over to the four-poster bed, sat down on the edge of the silk eiderdown, patted a place next to her inviting me to join her.

Kristin Scott Thomas.

CHAPTER EIGHT

My first day in heaven had been so wonderful that despite The Archangel Phil's warning of the danger of becoming bored with it all I spent the second day having another Saturday and doing exactly the same as I had on my first day. Manchester United thrashed Liverpool five-nil again (Hernandez, Rooney, Valencia (2), Vidic), I dined royally at Michael Caines *Abode* again, and I spent the night with Kristin Scott Thomas again. All three experiences were brilliant, especially the last.

My morning had been different. On the day I died I arrived in heaven around noon, so far as I could make out - I remember being taken down to the theatre at around eleven, so it all depended on how long it had taken the surgeon to butcher me to death and how much time the trip to heaven had taken up. My guess was more or less immediately after I'd died; there was the journey through the tunnel to be taken into consideration but that had taken next to no time.

So in the morning, and at a loose end, I needed to find something to do to fill in my time before the delights of the afternoon, evening and night to follow. The first hour had been easy. A leisurely full English breakfast provided by the Midland Hotel's excellent kitchens. Fruit juice, cornflakes, eggs, bacon, sausage, mushrooms, tomatoes, beans, fried bread, toast, coffee. Served at the table, silver service - the Midland apparently having no time for this help yourself from the buffet nonsense. The hotel was excellent in every way and I certainly wouldn't be busting a gut to find a place of my own, not as long as they served such tasty breakfasts every morning and Kristin Scott Thomas was in Room 242's four-poster every night.

After breakfast it was on to King Street for a little more shopping. Shirts, trousers, underwear from Armani (I had wondered at Kristin's preference in men's underpants and, unsure, had got half-a-dozen each of slips, boxers and Y-fronts); a lovely Nappa leather jacket (I'd always wanted a nice leather jacket) from Wrapped in Leather, another pair of shoes, loafers, this time from Hobbs; and a diamond necklace from Ernest Jones for Kristin.

The following day I did exactly the same again except that in the morning, instead of shopping, I visited Manchester's Central Library to see if they'd acquired any new publications that might be of interest to me since my last visit. They hadn't, so I spent an hour or so re-reading a couple of books I'd read before, *Where Have All the Flowers Gone?* an account of life and death in Auschwitz, and Adolf Hitler's *Mein Kampf*, yet again. Whilst leafing through the latter it occurred to me that I might well have been doing exactly the same thing if I'd still been on earth - or at least I might have been before the later stages of my cancer had confined me to bed. I had spent many hours at the library during the last two years of my life; being unemployed had its compensations as well as its disadvantages.

The difference was that when I'd spent my mornings in the earth version of the Central Library I wouldn't have breakfasted at the Midland, Manchester United wouldn't be hammering Liverpool five-nil that afternoon, I wouldn't be dining at Michael Caines *Abode* that evening, and I most certainly wouldn't be making love to Kristin Scott Thomas that night, and for a good half of it if last night is anything to go by.

The library was exactly the same as it was the last time I'd paid it a visit. It was just as though I was still alive. Over the years I'd got to know a few of the regulars, some to speak to and pass the time of day with, maybe have a coffee with in the basement cafe, others just nodding acquaintances. And they were all still there, just like before. Miss Jennings, one of the assistant librarians, a particularly friendly lady who occasionally helped me find a book I wished to refer to; Mr Galbraith, who knew almost as much about the Second World War as I did; Mr Bottomley, who shared my interest in Adolf Hitler's rise to power; and Herman the German, actually Klaus, Mr Streiger, with his strangulated half English/ half German way of speaking, and with whom I got on with as well as anyone despite him being on the other side. And they all treated me as though things were completely normal, as though it was just another day, as though nothing had happened. (It dawned on me only after I'd been in heaven a week or so, and back to the library a couple of times, that as far as they were concerned nothing *had* happened.)

"Good morning, Mr Smith. What may I help you with today?"

"Here Norman, did you know Winston Churchill had a big dick? Says here he did. I never knew that."

"They've got the name of Hitler's birthplace wrong. It was *Braunau am Inn*."

"Norman mein friend, kommen sie shit mit me and sprechen a vile."

But where everything at the library had been exactly the same, later, at The Old Goat Inn, nothing had been the same.

I had dropped in at The Old Goat Inn quite a few times

over the years. It used to be my kind of pub, traditional, beer from hand pumps, a dartboard, a domino table, cribbage, a decent pork pie to eat with your pint if you felt a bit peckish, spot on, what else would you want? Six months ago all that had changed. It had been 'modernised', been subjected to a 'makeover'. I couldn't believe my eyes when I saw what they'd done to it. Out on the pavement there'd been a notice: 'Real Ale Inside'. The ale might have been real but everything else inside was artificial; the plywood oak beams, the plastic topped 'wood effect' tables, the polystyrene stone walls, the smile on the barmaid's face. In short it was everything I don't like in a pub; pool tables, muzak, slot machines, games with mind-numbing sound effects played by numb-minded youths that involved much zapping of enemy spaceships and deafening explosions; you name it The Old Goat Inn had it, and all in open-plan horror so that there was no escape from the nightmare.

The real ale they advertised may well have been real but it was also the only ale, the remainder of the bar's six pumps being taken up by five different brands of lager, all of which probably tasted the same - a lager's individual popularity apparently being measured in depth of advertising coverage rather than depth of flavour.

The facsimile of a large, fat green grub, standing on the bar holding a menu, wittily, or so its creator must have imagined, informed the clientele that The Old Goat Inn did pub grub. The pub grub itself, which the menu proclaimed was 'clasically british' (sic) consisted of scampi, beef and ale pie (whether it was real ale wasn't indicated), moussaka, pizza, and three different curries. The vegetarian option was a vegetarian curry, which I wouldn't mind betting was any of the three different curries with the meat taken out.

Now, in heaven, I had only gone into the pub because I wanted to go the toilet and couldn't find one, Manchester, as is the case with most British city centres, boasting about as many public conveniences as the planet Saturn.

Inside the pub it had been a revelation. Gone were the pool tables, the muzak, the games, and all things artificial. Instead was everything I want in a pub; real oak beams, open coal fires, horse brasses and copper knick-knacks adorning the walls, sepia photographs of scenes of long ago, little alcoves where a man could enjoy a quiet pint and hear himself speak and be spoken to if he wanted to chat with a fellow drinker, and a barmaid who had been employed for her cheery but efficient manner rather than the size and visibility of her breasts. What was once a white ceiling was now brown, stained by the nicotine from all the cigarette smoking that was still allowed. Five of the bar's six pumps were used for real ale with the remaining one for lager, and the green grub holding the menu of 'clasical british food' had been replaced by a simple menu of good old-fashioned favourites, including ploughman's lunch.

As I ordered the Blue Stilton version of the Ploughman's and a pint of Theakston's Old Peculier to wash it down with (free, although everyone else paid) I made a mental note to question The Archangel Phil about the changes at The Old Goat Inn. How could it be? How could the pub have been totally transformed from what it had been, into what it was now, in the space of a month? If it had been taken over by another brewery and given a makeover they'd been sharp about it, and besides when that happened it was usually to install slot machines and juke boxes and plastic in various manifestations, not take them out.

I would also require my mentor to throw some light on

the strange occurrence the previous evening at Michael Caines *Abode*.

As with the two previous evenings the food was excellent. The restaurant was full and two minor 'celebrities' had been present; an actor from Coronation Street and a topless glamour model, although thankfully she wasn't topless at the moment, and even more thankfully the Coronation Street actor wasn't acting. Being a fan neither of soap operas nor topless models I didn't recognise either of the celebrities, and still wouldn't if the woman at the next table hadn't pointed them out to her husband. "You see him. He's Gail's new feller. Yes, another one, she never learns does she. Another murderer by the look of him. And the girl with him was Page Three in the Sport last week."

Not present at Michael Caine's *Abode* again was Michael Caine, but then I hadn't expected he would be. In fact I would have foregone the attendance of quite a few topless models and the entire cast of Coronation Street for an appearance by the famous actor, as he has always been one of my very favourite film stars.

I'd first seen the him - in fact it was the first time anyone had seen him on screen - in his debut film *Zulu*, and I'd been a huge fan ever since. *The Ipcress File*? Loved it. *Alfie*? Brilliant. While I was sipping my wine between courses I thought how nice it would be if he were to put in an appearance, how it would put the icing on the cake of my dining experience if he were to suddenly step through from the kitchens to greet his guests, and for some unexplained reason notice me amongst the diners and came over to say hello. "Hi there. Norman, isn't it?" he would say, and casually sit down at my table, drink a glass of wine with me and pass the time of day chatting about this and that. No sooner had the thought entered my head than Michael Caine did just that. Even down to calling me by name. It was all quite wonderful. He even related an amusing anecdote and at the end of it said: "Not a lot of people know that."

When he said it I thought I couldn't have been happier if Michael, acting the part of Lieutenant Gonville Bromhead, had suddenly stood up and shouted "Front rank fire! Second rank fire! Rear rank fire!" as he had done to telling and magnificent effect in *Zulu*. And in a flash, and to my great delight, what happened next in the film - wave upon wave of Zulu warriors throwing themselves on the guns of the beleaguered British outpost - happened in Michael Caine's *Abode*, and in about ten seconds flat the restaurant was knee deep in dead Africans, half the diners, two waiters, the sommelier, the Coronation Street actor and the topless glamour model.

CHAPTER NINE

On the following day I was in heaven. Both literally and metaphorically. As happy as a dog with two dicks. Following my meeting with the Archangel Phil I began to grow a third. The opportunity to live in a house once lived in by one of my all time favourite Manchester United footballers was the ultimate in dreams come true. It wasn't a golden ticket I'd been handed; this was the platinum ticket, with knobs on.

"And this is the master bedroom," The Archangel Phil had said.

David Beckham's old flat in Alderley Edge was the second of ex-Manchester United footballer's houses my mentor had taken me to view. Or rather I had taken my mentor to view, as I'd decided to give my new Mercedes SL Convertible 500 a run out to get the feel of it. It had felt very nice indeed.

Purchased at The Archangel Phil's suggestion earlier that morning at the Mercedes Manchester main dealership it had once again been acquired with the minimum of fuss and the absence of money.

I was sold on the car from the moment I visualised myself behind it's padded leather steering wheel, speeding along a country road, Kristin at my side, the wind in her hair. I would have been sold on a twenty-year-old Ford Fiesta with Kristin by my side with knits in her hair but it was icing on the cake time again; I was quickly learning that the words 'icing' and 'cake' were constant companions in this wonderful place called heaven.

"It's the bedroom that Becks and Posh would have slept in," continued The Archangel Phil. "They would have made love in here often, I would imagine," he added temptingly.

Far from tempting me the thought of coupling Beckhams was more likely to put me off. Although still a huge fan of David, despite him turning his back on United when he stopped becoming a footballer and became a fashion icon, I have no time at all for his wife. I once saw her described in a newspaper as an English Rose. I'd shaken my head in disbelief. Whoever said it had obviously confused lissom with gristle. Nor did English Roses have bottom lips that jutted out farther than the roof of one of the cantilever stands at Old Trafford. However The Archangel Phil's mentioning of Posh and Becks making love in the bedroom reminded me that I could soon be making love to Kristin in it, which immediately put it back on my wish list.

"What do you think to it then?" asked The Archangel Phil.

"I'm not sure." Making love to Kristin apart, I very much liked the spacious modern flat and the idea of living in Alderley Edge. Although the village is deep in the Cheshire countryside it is handy for town and only an hour away from the Derbyshire Dales, probably less in the new Merc. But I'd also been quite impressed by George Best's old house in nearby Bramhall. On entering George's bedroom The Archangel Phil had made the same remark he had when he entered David Beckham's bedroom, that George would very often have made love there with one of his girlfriends, maybe a Miss World or two, although he had left off the 'I would imagine', probably because around two thousand women and the whole of the football world had known it for a racing certainty.

A moment's thought brought me to a decision. "I'd like a look at Bobby Charlton's place."

"No problem."

An hour later found us entering Sir Bobby Charlton's master bedroom in Lymm, yet another pretty, unspoilt, Cheshire village. The Archangel Phil didn't mention it was the bedroom where Sir Bobby and his wife had often made love, for which I was grateful; George Best is long dead and David Beckham long gone but Sir Bobby is still very much alive and the thought of the seventy-four year old United legend getting his oats is not the dignified image I like to keep of my hero.

"So what do you think?" said the archangel, after I'd had a good look round.

Something puzzled me. "I know David Beckham doesn't live in Alderley Edge anymore." I said. "And Georgie Best doesn't live in Wilmslow. But Bobby Charlton still lives here; what will he do if I move in?"

"Bobby Charlton lives here on earth," said The Archangel Phil. "This is heaven."

I thought I understood. "So he won't still be living in it?"

The Archangel Phil affirmed this with a nod and said, "Bobby Charlton's house then? It's obvious you're very much taken by it."

I couldn't make up my mind. "I like the others too."

"Then why not have all three?"

Was he having me on? "All three?"

"You're in heaven."

If we hadn't had a chat before setting out I would have thought my mentor was joking. Not now though. I was quickly learning that just about anything was possible in heaven. Earlier I had asked about The Old Goat Inn.

"Think back to the time just before you went in," The Archangel Phil said. "What were you thinking?"

"That I was in need of a pee."

"Anything else?"

"Not that I can think of."

"You mentioned before that you were familiar with the pub. Is it possible you imagined how nice it would be if instead of being the pub from hell it was exactly the sort of pub you like?"

I thought about this for a moment. "I don't remember. I could have; it used to be that sort of pub."

"So you *wanted* it to be the sort of pub you like?"

"I suppose."

"Well there you are then?"

"What do you mean, there I am?"

"The assistants at the shops where you bought your new clothes - love the yellow waistcoat by the way - they treated you how you wanted to be treated?"

"Yes. Yes they did."

"They were like you wanted them to be?"

"Yes."

"Perhaps you'd had that thought before you entered the shop?"

"Probably. I can't be doing with the ones who can't be arsed to serve you. Or when they're all over you - 'Suits you, sir' - they're worse if anything."

"But they were neither dilatory nor overbearing?"

"No, they were spot on."

"And did Manchester United beat Liverpool five-nil?"

"Three times. Every day."

"And you've already mentioned your liaison with a

certain Miss Scott Thomas."

It was beginning to make sense. "You mean I just want something to happen and it happens?"

"Exactly that."

We were sat on the bench in Piccadilly Gardens where we'd first met. Nearby a man was trying to sell passers-by copies of the *Big Issue*. As usual he would probably have had more success if he'd been trying to sell them AIDS. I picked up on this.

"What's all that about then? A *Big Issue* seller in heaven?"

"He's not in heaven. Well not his heaven. He's in your heaven."

"How do you mean?"

"Everyone's heaven is different. Everyone who dies has a heaven of their own."

"Their own heaven?"

"It only makes sense when you think about; no two people are alike, none of us enjoy exactly the same things. You are in the heaven that is 'heaven' to you, your very own heaven."

"With *Big Issue* sellers in it?" I shook my head. "I don't think so. Why would I want *Big Issue* sellers in my heaven? I feel sorry for the poor buggers."

The Archangel Phil frowned. "Maybe I could have explained it better." He took a moment before carrying on, then said, "As with all new arrivals I started you off in the world you left behind. A world in which you are completely familiar, so that the shock isn't too great. There were *Big Issue* sellers in your life on earth so there are *Big Issue* sellers in your life in heaven. That's how things were and how they are at this moment. But once you've had time to settle in, once you've had a good look round, you'll be able to change things so that your heaven is just how you want it to be; how things will be in your heaven from now on and for evermore. Do you see?"

I let it all sink. "Right. I think."

"Excellent."

"Well I certainly don't want any *Big Issue* sellers in my heaven."

"So get rid of them."

"How?"

"Simply by not wanting them to be in it."

"Right." I shut my eyes tight shut in concentration.

"You don't have to close your eyes. You just want it and that's the way it is."

I opened my eyes. The *Big Issue* seller had disappeared.

The Archangel Phil smiled what I was beginning to think of as that smile of his. "Just like that."

"Magic."

"No, heaven."

I still couldn't quite believe it. "And I can get rid of *anybody*? Tramps, beggars, down-and- outs, anybody else who's having a rough time, everybody I feel sorry for?"

"It's entirely up to you."

I realised something. "*That* explains what happened at Michael Caine's. I *wanted* it to happen."

"I'm sorry?"

I explained Michael Caine's sudden appearance and what had followed.

"The proof of the pudding," said The Archangel Phil.

I thought of something. "Can I have people who have died in my heaven?"

"A lot of people ask that. You're probably thinking of a

loved one, your mother perhaps?"

"No!" I moved on quickly lest The Archangel Phil started trying to talk me into it. "I was thinking more John Lennon."

"How about George Harrison too?"

"Really?"

"Of course. You can have anyone at all. Groucho Marx has Hitler in his heaven."

"Go on?" I shook my head in disbelief. "I'd have thought Hitler was the last person Groucho Marx would want in his heaven."

"He has him living in a house between two families of Jews. Has him tearing his hair out by all accounts."

This latest news brought out the worst in me. "Can I have Graham Norton living between two homophobes?"

"I believe quite a few people are doing that already."

I grinned at this. "I think I'm going to like it here."

"I'm sure you are," said The Archangel Phil, then raised a finger of warning. "But just as soon as you stop enjoying yourself be sure to let me know and I'll arrange for you to go back."

I gaped at him. "Back? Are you joking? Why would I want to go back?"

"Most people do, eventually. It not very often there isn't a waiting list for reincarnation." My expression must have told The Archangel Phil that I found this very hard to believe. He said, "It's true. People get fed up with enjoying themselves all the time once the novelty has worn off. It's the familiarity breeds contempt thing; what is very enjoyable becomes commonplace when you're doing it all the time. No highs and lows you see. Nothing to look forward to."

"I can do without the lows," I said with feeling. "I had more than a bellyful of lows when I was alive."

"I'm just giving you fair warning. If you're intent on staying here for eternity take my advice and find yourself an occupation. Something to occupy your mind, bring a sense of purpose to your existence. Even then I wouldn't like to guarantee anything, even that might not be enough to stop you wanting to go back sooner or later; Jehovah's Witnesses put their names down for reincarnation in a matter of weeks."

This really opened my eyes. "Really? I thought they'd love it in heaven; they're always going on about how wonderful it's going to be."

"Oh it's wonderful for them all right. At first. Every door they knock on they get a convert. Their idea of heaven you see. But then the people who they talk into becoming Jehovah's Witnesses start knocking on doors and talk even more people into becoming Jehovah's Witnesses and before you know it everyone in their heaven is a Jehovah's Witness and there's nothing for them to do." I laughed at the wonderful irony of this. The Archangel Phil went on. "Vicars and other men of the cloth can't wait to get back either. They want everyone to believe in God you see, and when they do their churches are packed out, there aren't enough pews, standing room only, people come to blows to get a seat, children are trampled underfoot in the rush to get in, it's absolute mayhem. I've seen people hanging from the steeple before now. Very soon the vicars and priests and rabbis can't take any more of the aggro. No, as I was saying Norman, it's the ones who carry on working once they're here who tend to stay forever. It gives them something to do, something to occupy their minds. As a man needs a purpose in life so does he need a purpose in life after death."

CHAPTER TEN

SCENE 17. DAY. BACKROOM, BADA BING.

TONY, PAULIE, SILVIO, RALPHIE and *CHRISTOPHER* *are seated at the table playing poker. A large pile of dollars in the centre of the table. PAULIE, supremely confident that he holds the winning hand, lays his cards on the table. He looks keenly at TONY inviting him to do the same. As he sees the cards, TONY looks sick. PAULIE smirks. TONY dismally lays his cards on the table one at a time. First a queen, then another queen. Then, after a pause, playing to the gallery with a grin, he lays down another queen. PAULIE is crushed.*

PAULIE:
Moth....er....fucker! Three cocksucking bitches! I must have pissed on a Bishop!

TONY laughs as he wraps an arm around the pile of money. CHRISTOPHER, SILVIO and RALPHIE join in the laughter, enjoying the moment.

TONY:
(RAKING IN THE MONEY) Come to Uncle Tony.

They all laugh at PAULIE'S expense. TONY gets up, stuffing money into his pockets.

TONY:
I gotta go. (TO CHRISTOPHER) Weren't you supposed to be seeing that union guy in north Jersey this morning?

CHRISTOPHER:
I'm already there, T.

TONY:
And try not to fuck up this time.

CHRISTOPHER:
Jesus I said I'm sorry. If it hadn't of been for....

TONY:
(CUTTING IN) Save it. You can't put the shit back in the donkey. But remember - I don't want Johnny Sac and that cocksucker Phil to know anything about this. So not a word to anybody.

CHRISTOPHER:
I am a Trappist monk.

PAULIE:
What the fuck is a Trappist monk?

SILVIO:
A Silent Order. Keep their traps shut all the time. Motherfuckers never say a word.

PAULIE:
I got a wife like that.

RALPHIE:
I got a wife never shuts up; what sort of a monk you call that?

CHRISTOPHER:
A trap monk.

They all laugh. The door opens. CARLO pops his head round.

CARLO:
Guy to see you, Tone. Wouldn't give his name. Says he wants to surprise you.

TONY:
Well tell Mr No Name that Tony Soprano don't like surprises.

CARLO:
(TURNS TO SPEAK TO SOMEONE OUT OF VISION) The boss says he don't like....

ENGLISH NORMAN enters, pushes CARLO out of the way.

ENGLISH NORMAN:
Shift, punk.

TONY recognises ENGLISH NORMAN immediately, is delighted.

TONY:
(DELIGHTED) There he is! Moth....er....fucker!

None of the others recognise the visitor.

RALPHIE:
You know this guy, Tony?

TONY:
English Norman. I met him in London when I was over there.
a while ago.

As they've been talking ENGLISH NORMAN has stepped
forward. TONY goes to meet him halfway. They embrace,
backslapping each other in the time-honoured Mafia way,
then look fondly at each other at arm's length.

TONY:
(TO THE OTHERS) This guy has the canal barge business
tied up tighter than a rattlesnake's ass. Owns half the canal
barges in England.

ENGLISH NORMAN:
(TO THE OTHERS) If any of you guys ever want a canal
barge, I'm your man.

RALPHIE:
Cocksucker shoulda tied up the speedboat business, I mighta
taken him up on the offer. What the fuck would I want with a
canal barge?

ENGLISH NORMAN:
You could maybe use it as your coffin.

RALPHIE:
What's that you say?

ENGLISH NORMAN takes out a handgun

ENGLISH NORMAN:
Say your prayers, Arsehole.

ENGLISH NORMAN coolly shoots RALPHIE through the forehead.

Keeping TONY and the others covered he backs for the door, reaches behind him for the handle, goes out, closes the door behind him.

TONY, SILVIO, PAULIE, CHRISTOPHER, CARLO:
Moth....er....fucker!

The credits rolled. I waited until the caption '*Special Guest Norman Smith as English Norman*' rolled past then reached for the remote and switched off the TV set. I was quite pleased with my performance and thought that I might be Jimmy McNulty's new partner Norman 'Nicker' Smith in *The Wire* next time out.

I was in the TV room of Bobby Charlton's house in Lymm - rather than live in the houses of all three United legends, as The Archangel Phil had suggested I might, I plumped for just one as I didn't want to appear greedy. Bobby's wife Norma has a nice taste in furniture and decor and I hardly had to change a thing. I was especially taken by the ornate white conservatory furniture, made from the bleached bones of deceased Manchester City supporters, or at least that's what a small plaque embedded in the glass table top informed me. The Charlton's house was by no means the only thing I have added to my heaven, or changed in it, during the last couple of weeks.

The first thing I changed was the score line at Old Trafford. Now it's sometimes six or seven-nil to United. Once, when I got carried away, it was sixteen-nil. Twice it has been just one-nil. The one-nil victories were my favourites. Not for the score, which in normal circumstances be disappointing - even for a less rabid supporter than me - but for the manner in which it is achieved. The match unfurls not with United doing ninety per cent of the attacking and completely outplaying Liverpool, as per usual, but exactly the opposite. For the whole ninety minutes. For most of those minutes, from my position just to the right of the section of the north stand reserved for 'away' spectators, I watch the Liverpool fans as much as I watch the match. Their faces are a mixture of agony and ecstasy; the ecstasy brought about by their team completely outplaying the hated enemy, the agony through hitting the woodwork seventeen times and missing eight penalties whilst doing it. In contrast my face has a permanent smile. They don't know what's coming. I do.

With just ten seconds of injury time to go the agony and ecstasy on the faces of the Liverpool supporters has been replaced with contented smiles. All right, they hadn't managed to beat United, but they had achieved a moral victory, they had completely outplayed them, made fools out of them, showed the arrogant bastards from the other end of the East Lancs Road how the game should be played.

Then, with three seconds of twelve minutes disputed injury time to go and Sir Alex on the touchline tapping his watch and giving the fourth official the hair-drier treatment, a hopeful ball into the Liverpool penalty area is met by Steven Gerard, who takes a huge lunge at it and with the last kick of the match slices it into the back of his own net. The referee blows the final whistle; there isn't even time to re-start the game. The Liverpool fans are absolutely devastated. Even more devastated than when United stuck sixteen goals past them. I love it. Glory in it. I feel a bit ashamed of myself for feeling the way I do but not so ashamed that I won't be doing it again, and often.

I didn't feel ashamed about it when I got rid of all the branches of McDonalds, the very first of the changes I made to my heaven.

I have only once eaten a Big Mac in my life, one being a chastening enough experience to risk ever eating another. I don't like anything about Big Macs. I don't like the look of them, I don't like the smell of them, I especially don't like the taste of them and it never ceases to amaze me how anyone could like them. There is maybe an excuse for children liking them because their taste buds haven't fully developed but for an adult to allow a Big Mac into his mouth without being force fed is a notion quite beyond my apprehension. I don't care over much for McDonalds as a company either. I don't like the way they proliferate, like boils; how they seem to just appear overnight to fill a previously empty space, or, if an empty space is unavailable, how something will be knocked down to make it available, so that nowadays you can't travel a mile in any direction without coming across one unless you happen to be on top of Ben Nevis, and I wouldn't put it past them sticking one up there before much longer; and I don't like the way McDonalds all look exactly the same, the garish design of their outsides, with the Golden M, the over-bright over-colourful plastic noisy insides; the sheer McDonaldness of them.

Before getting rid of all the McDonalds I asked myself if I was being fair to everyone. All right, I reasoned, it is my own heaven and I can do with it just as I like, and nothing would please me more than if there were no branches of McDonalds in it, but what about everyone else living in my heaven? How would they feel about it? I have never had objections to other people liking McDonalds - one man's meat is another man's McDonalds - so instead of depriving others of them I could simply carry on trying to ignore them, as I did on earth. However when I mentioned it to The Archangel Phil he explained that if I got rid of them it would only be in my own heaven that there would be an absence of McDonalds, as would be the case with any other things I got rid of. So I did what I had to do with a clear conscience. Much happier in the knowledge that any changes I made would only affect my own heaven I quickly added Kentucky Fried Chicken and Burger King to McDonalds then set about making more changes that would make my heaven a happier place than it was already.

The first thing to go was royalty; not only a drain on society to my way of thinking but one whose bloodline was nearer to Hitler's than mine and therefore especially deserving of the chop. The rest of the aristocracy quickly followed, along with all politicians, merchant bankers, lawyers and financial advisers.

My disillusionment with the world before I departed it was pretty total; even so I was surprised at the number of things I hadn't liked about it. Well over a hundred. Taking immense pleasure in my work I got rid of them one by one and in next to no time had done away with litter, dog shit, automated phone systems, phone sales, lads who walk about with their jeans round their hips showing about six inches of their underpants, girls showing a similar amount of thong, unmarried teenage mothers pushing prams about, Harry Potter, Radio One, litter, Coca-Cola, dog shit (especially), queue jumpers, Bono, mobile phones on trains - as the owner of a posh Mercedes I didn't visualise that I'd be doing much travelling on trains but wanted to free other rail passengers of this nuisance - fat people in velour jogging suits, thin people in velour jogging suits, velour, junk mail, people who make a noise when they're eating, personalised number plates except for 1 TIT, cyclists who cycle up your inside when you're waiting at traffic lights, small yapping dogs, tailgaters, cold callers, hot gospellers, telesales people and celebrity fitness DVDs. And the word 'Gay' now means happy and carefree again and not homosexual.

Then I set about television. Channel Five had gone in its entirety. All Soaps went, along with all makeover shows, talent shows - along with the expression "You nailed it" - reality shows, victim shows and all other shows attended by studio audiences that consist of a hand-picked collection of imbeciles caught in traps coming out of Lidl. All shows with the word 'Celebrity' in the title were summarily axed. All the brain dead game shows had gone, with the exception of *Total Wipeout*, which I re-named *Total Crap* and kept in the schedules to annoy me on one of my bad days. All other dumbed-down shows disappeared. Adverts joined them. Likewise Noel Edmonds, Graham Norton, Alan Carr, Jonathan Ross, Chris Evans, Danny Baker, Russell Brand, Jeremy Clarkson, his two scruffy sidekicks on *Top Gear*, *Top Gear*, Cheryl Cole, Katie Price, Davina McCall, Kerry

Katona, Carol Vorderman, her equally shouty sisters on Loose Women and loose women. Plus any programme starring an actor doing something they hadn't become famous for, fed to the viewers on the conceit that because Martin Clunes or Griff Rhys Jones or someone else who should know better is doing it it will be more be interesting than if someone you'd never heard of was doing it - *Robson Green goes Clog Dancing, Stephen Tomkinson goes Brass Rubbing, Tamsin Outhwaite goes Robson Green and Stephen Tomkinson Rubbing.* However I hadn't got rid of Bruce Forsyth. Not just yet. I contented myself with merely publicly stripping him of his knighthood on live TV so he'd know what it felt like to be humiliated in public. I would banish him from my heaven later, at my leisure and pleasure.

A problem resulting from my purge on TV was that once I'd got rid of everything I didn't like there was very little left apart from sport, *Flog It*, repeats of *Rising Damp* and *Dad's Army* and a few documentaries. I mentioned this to The Archangel Phil the next time we met.

"Well what sort of programmes do you enjoy?" he asked me.

"*Seinfeld. Curb Your Enthusiasm. The Wire.* But they're not on any more. And *The Sopranos* of course. I used to love *The Sopranos*, the best thing on TV ever for my money; that isn't on any more either."

The Archangel Phil hadn't seen this as a problem. "So have it on."

"What? On DVD you mean? Well I suppose. But I've already seen every episode about ten times; even *The Sopranos* can get a bit boring when you've seen it that often."

"So have some new episodes."

"What? What do you mean?"

"You're in heaven."

After a moment's delay while the penny dropped I said, still not able to believe my luck, "You mean I only have to want there to be more *The Sopranos* and there will be more *The Sopranos*?"

"You can be IN *The Sopranos*."

Initially, as the only acting experience I've ever had is acting the goat, I was going to be a corpse, a 'stiff' as they call them in the States, a candidate for a concrete coffin. Then it dawned on me that all I need do was to 'want' to be a good actor and I would be a good actor. And so it turned out. I was actually up for an 'Emmy' for Best Supporting Actor. And I'd have got it if I 'wanted' to but I didn't want to go through the trauma of doing an acceptance speech.

Before leaving to put in my appearance in *The Sopranos* I had filled in The Archangel Phil about some of the things I'd rid my heaven of.

"Poverty. There's no poverty now. Neither in this country nor abroad. Africa especially. No more starving Africans. No more kids with swollen bellies and flies in their eyes. I've got rid of Mugabe too. He's no longer around to make his countrymen's life a bloody misery. And Omar Al-bashir and Gadaffi and all the other African dictators I could think of. And that Korean nutcase, Kim whatnot, he won't be doing any more of his evil."

The Archangel Phil smiled. "Good for you, Norman, that's the idea. I'm sure you'll do very well here."

CHAPTER ELEVEN

And so it turned out. The huge burden that had weighed heavily on my shoulders for the last few months before my death had been lifted and I walked as if on air. I had a wonderful life to look forward to which, while not technically life, was something far better than any life I could ever have even hoped for had I remained fit and well on earth.

Following the *Zulu* incident at Michael Caine's *Abode*, and not wanting any more deaths on my hands, I was now extra careful about exactly what I 'wanted'. I managed to avoid another disaster - apart from the time I wanted the Queen's horse to fall at the final fence in the Grand National when half a mile in the lead, which it duly did, but in doing so caused its jockey to break his neck when he fell heavily. Thankfully I discovered that all I had to do was to want his neck to heal itself and that's what would happen. So there was no harm done. (Except to the Queen's hopes of saddling the winner of the Grand National of course, which was the object of the exercise.)

After six successive Saturdays my days had now settled into a conventional pattern of weeks of Sundays to Saturdays. My past life, my life on earth, seemed light years away instead of just weeks. All my days were wonderful. My fourth Tuesday in heaven was especially wonderful; the sun was shining, the birds were singing, the fragrance of sweet-smelling flowers filled the air, I had the beginnings of a Mediterranean tan, my hair was growing back nicely, I was looking years younger and Kristin had just given me my first ever blow job.

I felt a bit guilty about the blow job in much the same way I felt guilty about Man U being outplayed by Liverpool only to end up winning in the last seconds; although, as with the football, not guilty enough to stop me having further blow jobs. I 'wanted' her to do it of course, and wondered if, left to her own devices, she would perform this wonderful form of sex on me in the normal course of events. I thought I might find out sometime. But not for the moment.

By then I was deeply in love with Kristin. She was aged just 23 when I'd seen her in her second film, *Under the Cherry Moon,* and had first become aware of her. She was quite beautiful then, and now, at the age of fifty, had lost none of her beauty. She was all I ever wanted in a woman and now the wanting was over. Sex with her was fantastic. Much, much better than any sex I'd had before. Not that I'd ever had much, and what bit I did have wasn't very frequent and often furtive, due to the surroundings in which it took place, usually outdoors in the park or in a bus shelter, and on one occasion on the back seat of Piggy Higginbottom's car; this last an even more furtive fuck than usual as Piggy refused to vacate the driver's seat whilst I was having it.

I looked at Kristin by my side, gave a huge sigh of content and counted my blessings.

I spared a thought, not for the first time, for my fellow patients in the cancer ward back on earth. If they only knew what I knew they'd be telling the doctors where they could stick their 'chemo', they'd be getting the whole sorry business over with and joining me in heaven. Well in their own heavens. Instead they'd still be subjecting themselves daily to all manner of humiliations in the hope of eking out a bit more low quality time on earth. Hanging on to life like limpets when they'd be far better off jumping off the end of a cliff like lemmings.

Kristin broke into my thoughts. "You've changed, Norman," she said. She was propped up on an elbow looking critically at me.

We were sharing a post-coital Marlborough cigarette. ('Smoking Kills' packets of cigarettes were not to be had in my heaven, I'd soon seen to that. I had briefly toyed with the idea of having them replaced with 'Smoking Might Very Well Kill But Who Gives A Shit You're Better Off Dead' cigarettes but in the end decided they should simply revert to their former names as my proposed name wouldn't all go on the packet in big enough letters for anyone to see it.

"How do you mean changed, Kristin?" I said to my love.

"You're so much more confident than when we first met. Much more at ease. More comfortable. Both with yourself and with me. Especially with me."

"Am I?" The question was disingenuous; I knew she was right. Sleeping on a regular basis with one of the world's most beautiful women, seeing the envious looks of other men when we were out together, had done wonders for my self-esteem. Being freed from all the worries I'd had over the last few years of my life hadn't done much harm either.

"That first night." She smiled, recalling it. "I thought I was never going to get you into bed. Now I can hardly keep you out of it."

I was immediately concerned. "It's not too much for you is it? I mean I'm not being too greedy?"

She smiled and pecked me on the cheek. "You're just perfect, Norman darling."

I rolled over to face her. I could have lived in her eyes.

"Oh well in that case." I reached out for her.

She squealed and slipped deftly out of bed, snorted with laughter as I was left grabbing thin air. Safe from horny old me she said, "We should do something this morning."

"That was the idea."

"I mean *other* than making love again."

"Right."

"Any suggestions?"

"I'll leave it to you, darling." I used to think it was soppy when people called each other 'Darling'. Not any more. Not now I had Kristin.

"What's the weather like?" She went to the window and looked anxiously up at the sky.

She was living with me now. For my first few days in heaven I'd only seen her at night, when I got back to the Midland after football and food, then later at Bobby Charlton's house. But living with her was what I really wanted and of course whatever I wanted I got. I courted her first, not because I had to but because I thought it was the right thing to do. Kristin allowed herself to be courted, seemed to enjoy being courted, and when I thought I'd courted her for long enough I asked her to move in with me, and she agreed. Job done properly.

By then we'd been together for almost a month. There had only been one minor blip; when I asked her what her next film was going to be. A few times, with my encouragement, she had reminisced about some of her many film roles, the fun or otherwise she'd had whilst making them. As a long time film fan I enjoyed listening to her behind-the-scenes tales. I especially liked her talking about my favourite of her films, *The English Patient*, the film in which she first exposed her enchanted forest of pubic hair, a sight I had since pictured in my mind's eye a thousand times and could now, wonderfully, picture without recourse to memory.

But not once had she mentioned any future plans. When I brought up the subject she told me she had no idea what she'd be doing next; she was having a lovely time with me, she might take a bit of a break from films altogether for a while, she was in no rush to get back. I suspected that the only reason she wasn't in any rush to get back was because that was the way I wanted it to be.

*

The Archangel Phil confirmed this when I met up with him a day or two later.

"So if I want her to start making films again she will?"

"It's entirely up to you. Whatever you wish. You are...."

"....in heaven. I know."

"I believe Mr Brownlow's Kristin Scott Thomas hasn't made a film for fifteen years."

I blinked in surprise. "What?"

"Mr Brownlow's Kristin."

"Mr Brownlow's Kristin?"

"Another chap I mentored. He's seeing Miss Scott Thomas too."

"Seeing her? What do you mean, seeing her?"

"Living with her. At least I think he is. He was the last I heard; they have a place in Nice, near the *Promenade des Anglais*."

To say I was flabbergasted is putting it mildly. "But....I mean he can't be; she's living with me."

The Archangel Phil smiled patiently. "There are literally millions of men in heaven, Norman. Each one of them in his own heaven. Surely you don't think you're the only one amongst them who wants Kristin Scott Thomas as a girlfriend?"

It had never even entered my head. When it did I wished it hadn't, it was a thought I could have done without. My next thought was even worse. I voiced it. "Are there any more of them?"

"More?"

"Men seeing Kristin?"

"Well of course."

I hardly dared ask. "How many?"

The Archangel Phil shrugged. "It's hard to say exactly. I'd have to check. But well over a thousand. Miss Scott Thomas is a very desirable woman."

It was a chastening experience for me to be informed that the English Rose of my dreams was the heaven bicycle and for over a week I found it difficult to come to terms with. During this time I didn't see Kristin at all. At first I wasn't sure if I'd ever see her again. Then I thought I'd maybe send her off to make another film while I sorted my head out. Then I changed my mind and decided I'd try to forget about it. I tried to forget but couldn't .

The first night without her, alone in bed, I almost forsook her completely and wished that Helena Bonham Carter was between the sheets with me. But then I thought better of it. Wouldn't it be the same story? Wouldn't Miss Bonham Carter have to be shared with a thousand other lovers? With that cheeky little face of hers and pert bottom she was almost as desirable as Kristin.

In the end I just accepted it. After all it was unlikely I would see any of the thousand odd other men with their Kristin, in fact, when I came to think about it, it was impossible, because I would never 'want' that to happen;

things didn't happen in your heaven if you didn't want them to. Or that's what I thought.

*

Now, standing at the window of Bobby Charlton's (and mine) house in Lymm, Kristin said: "Well the weather's fine at the moment. I was going to suggest a drive to the Lakes? Perhaps have lunch at a lovely little pub I know near Keswick, *The Anchor* I think it's called, or *The Compass*, something nautical anyway." The prospect pleased her and she warmed to it. "We could go up Latrigg; that would be lovely. Have you ever climbed Latrigg?"

"Only once," I said, with a grimace. I had bad memories of Latrigg.

*

A neighbour had told my mother how nice Latrigg was. How wonderful the views were. My mother wasn't having that, she didn't have to put up with the neighbours telling her how nice being up Latrigg was, she wanted to go up Latrigg to find out how nice it was for herself. I pointed out to her that she was in no condition to climb a small mountain. Mother, however, had done her research. You could drive more than three quarters of the way up it, she informed me. I could carry her the rest of the way. And I did. Piggyback. About a mile. Most of the way with her telling me to shift my fool head out of the way, she couldn't see anything, I made a better door than a window. On reaching the top, exhausted, I set her down. She took one look at the view, which many believe to be the finest in the whole of the Lake District if not the world, said it was "No better than the view you get in Heaton Park" and told me to take her back down, anyway she was hungry. I told her I'd booked a boat trip for us on Lake Windermere. She cursed me.

*

At the window Kristin looked anxiously for rainclouds. "If it turns out like it did yesterday there won't be much point, we wouldn't see very much."

"Oh it'll be a beautiful day," I said confidently. "I've ordered it specially."

I wasn't joking. I decided what the weather was going to be like every day. Until yesterday each day of my time in heaven had been a beautiful, sunny day. Yesterday it had teemed down with rain. All day, stair rods, cats and dogs without let up. For yesterday I wanted it to be a bad day.

*

Although The Archangel Phil had told me that almost everyone who came to heaven wanted to return to earth sooner or later I just couldn't see it happening to me; in fact I don't think he would have said it if he'd known fully about the rotten time I'd had before I died. Even so I was mindful of what he'd said about enjoying myself too much; that it was all very well enjoying yourself but if you did it too often you'd soon get blasé about it, which would eventually lead to discontentment.

Where I could easily see that this might apply to other people I found it difficult to imagine it would happen to me. Besides, with my luck I'd probably end up with the sort of life I'd had on the two previous occasions. Or even worse. What if I were to go back as somebody like Mr Swindells, with his Huntington's Chorea? Or a starving African? Or, worse, a Liverpool supporter? Life wouldn't be worth living. So to guard against it ever happening I'd come up with a plan. My idea was simplicity itself. Every few days or so I would have a bad day. Then, having had the bad day, I would return refreshed for yet more wonderful days.

113

Yesterday had been my first bad day. And it had been truly awful.

After getting up and using the lavatory only to find there was no toilet paper and tripping up and cracking my head on the washbasin when on my way to the airing cupboard for another toilet roll whilst trying to hold up my trousers I completed my ablutions only to discover there were no eggs for breakfast. I love my boiled egg every morning (now the finest quality free-range of course), so went out to get half a dozen, but on the way back it suddenly started pouring down with rain. In my hurry to get home I dropped the box of eggs and trod on them, breaking all six. By then I was absolutely soaked to the skin and returned home eggless and in a foul mood and had my first ever row with Kristin.

The rest of the morning was one disaster after another. I banged my thumb with a hammer whilst putting up a picture, as soon as I'd got the picture up it fell down, the glass shattered, I cut my finger clearing it up and I couldn't find a plaster. Kristin had gone out "To get away from you if that's the sort of mood you're in", the doorbell had rung, I'd gone to answer it dripping blood only to find about a hundred Jehovah's Witnesses at the door waving Watchtowers.

Thereafter it was downhill all the way. It eventually stopped raining and at a loose end I went for a drive in the country in my new Maserati. I hadn't gone a mile when the rain started up again, worse than ever, now accompanied by a howling gale. A minute later I started with toothache and, distracted by the pain, ran the Maserati into the back of a Ford Mondeo. The Mondeo's driver, a slaphead with 'Liverpool Forever' tattooed on his forehead, jumped out of his car, wrenched open the door of the Maserati, called me a fucking stupid twat, hauled me bodily out of the car and punched me on the jaw. Believing my jaw to be broken I drove myself to hospital where I spent the next six hours waiting in A&E sat between to a woman with two crying babies, one of which vomited over me, and a down-and-out with BO. When the doctor finally saw me I was told I hadn't got a broken jaw but had got nits, probably from the down-and-out with BO. By the time I got home, having been deloused, Kristin was back. She kissed me and said the row was all her fault, she should have been more understanding. I told her not to be silly, it was my fault. She said that she was a least partially to blame. I said no she wasn't. She said yes she was and we continued bickering about whose fault it was and ended up having another full-scale row. She sulked all evening. I watched television. There was another episode of *The Sopranos* on. I wasn't in it but Ant and Dec were. Dec shot Tony Soprano and Ant shot shit. I turned it off and went to bed. Kristin followed about an hour later. I apologised to her. She accepted my apology. She got into bed. I kissed her tenderly. She smiled that sexy smile of hers. I asked her if she'd like to make love. She said she'd love to but she'd got her period. I made a mental note that I would probably only need a bad day every few weeks rather than every few days, put out the light and went to sleep.

*

But today things were back to normal and I had a much better time in the Lake District than the last time I'd visited it, mainly because when taking in the breathtaking views from the top of Latrigg my breath hadn't already been taken by virtue of having to carrying my mother up it. The views were even more breathtaking with Kristin by my side, almost as breathtaking as the views of Kristin.

CHAPTER TWELVE

The following day I asked The Archangel Phil if there was any way in which I could get in touch with the patients in the cancer ward back on earth. I wanted to tell them to stop trying to hang on to life and get themselves up to heaven and start enjoying themselves.

"I'm afraid not," The Archangel Phil said. "Not even God himself can do that."

This surprised me to say the least. "What? I thought God could speak to people? People *say* they speak to God."

"They're just deluding themselves. I blame the bible. It's meant to be allegorical but people take it literally. People with no imagination. Or too much of the wrong sort of imagination."

The Archangel Phil showed no signs of enlarging on this so I asked him to.

"Well take praying. People pray to God and sometimes they get what they pray for. But if you think about it they're bound to sometimes, law of averages. Yet they believe the reason they got what they prayed for is because God has answered their prayers. They conveniently overlook all the times he doesn't."

"Like they fool themselves into believing it?"

The Archangel Phil nodded. "Then you get a few unexplainable, inexplicable events - Lourdes is a prime example - mix the so-called miracles of Jesus into the myth and you've got religion."

"What do you mean 'so-called' miracles? "

"Turn water into wine? Bring people back from the dead?" The Archangel Phil shook his head. "They happened of course, but they weren't miracles, just illusions, tricks. Jesus was just an illusionist, the world's first stage magician."

I smiled, fully vindicated. "I always knew miracles were a load of old bollocks."

"God sent his 'Only Son' to perform the 'miracles' in order to impress people, so that they'd believe in him and by extension believe in God in heaven and a life beyond. Their reward for leading a good life. But as far as people talking to God and God answering them? Well you have to be in heaven to do that."

My ears pricked. "You can talk to God when you're in heaven?"

"Well naturally; I mean he's here isn't he."

"So I could talk to him if I wanted to?"

"Well of course."

"How would I go about that?"

"You just speak to him."

"Where?"

"Anywhere. God is everywhere."

"Can you see him?"

"No, he doesn't have a physical presence. Those pictures of a big head in the sky with curly hair and a beard are just fanciful illusions."

I came to a decision. "I'm going to talk to him. I'm going to ask him why he allows people to suffer before they die, because I've never been able to fathom that."

"Oh I can tell you that," said The Archangel Phil disarmingly, "He...."

I cut him off. "No, I prefer to hear it from the horse's

117

mouth."

The Archangel Phil shrugged. "Suit yourself. But he'll only tell you what I'd tell you."

*

So it came to pass that Norman spake unto God. First he asked Him why people had to die. And God said, "There must be deaths, Norman. If everyone were to live forever the world would soon become overpopulated. Famine and Pestilence and a great suffering of multitudes would follow in its wake and verily the Earth would perish."

And Norman spake and said, "Yes, that's all very well, but why do you allow them to suffer before they die?"

"I don't," replied God. "For there is but nothing I can do about it."

This shocked Norman and he thought deeply on it. He had expected The Lord God Almighty to defend himself, to tell him that He allowed people to suffer in order to test their faith, as the Jehovah's Witnesses had claimed. After a while he said, "So what is your purpose here then?"

And God said, "Verily, when people die I provide a home for them in heaven."

And this disappointed Norman greatly and a great sadness came over him and he said, "Is that all?"

And God said, "It is sufficient for most."

And Norman was quick to reassure God, saying "Oh it is. More than enough. It's just that....well I....well not me, some people....are under the impression that you do a lot more."

And God said, "No, I just do heaven. I hope thou are not too disappointed?"

And Norman said, "No. Far from it. No, it'll do me." And Norman went happily on his way.

Amen.

CHAPTER THIRTEEN

Following my conversation with God I felt a lot less guilty about not believing in him when I was on earth. Not that I'd felt all that guilty in the first place. Besides, I'd been right in a way, there wasn't a God in the way that religious fanatics, Jehovah's Witnesses and the like believed there was; that you only have to believe in him and that would be the end of all your problems, that you only had to pray to him and everything would be all right. The way things really are, that he is just the host of a sort of gigantic free pleasureland, makes much more sense to my way of thinking.

So with that out of the way it was with a clear conscience I got on with my wonderful existence. And with nothing to do but enjoy myself I got to thinking that it might be a good idea to start working through the list of things I'd planned to do before I died but wasn't able to get round to doing due to the chemotherapy. When I mentioned it to Kristin she was all for it, especially when I told her we'd be going to the West of Scotland; she loved that part of the country, had friends there, we could drop in on them.

We started off at *Le Manoir aux Quatre Saisons* as I didn't count the time on earth when I'd almost been sick over Raymond Blanc's signature dish.

*

This time Raymond Blanc himself was in attendance. I wanted him to be. After we had finished our meal - another of Monsieur Blanc's signature dishes, absolutely mouth-watering - *Le patron* himself came over to our table, sat with us, chatted and shared magnum of *Pol Roger*. I wanted him to. Unfortunately I forgot to want Raymond to speak in a manner in which I had a sporting chance of understanding what the hell he was talking about so missed the first two minutes of the Frenchman's bonhomie before I realised my error. (I think the man at the BBC who thought up the title *Raymond Blanc's Kitchen Secrets* for the chef's last TV series must have done it for a joke as the vast majority of the secrets remained secret thanks to Raymond's mangling of the English language.) After I'd put this right I found Monsieur Blanc to be an exceptionally charming host, full of interesting anecdotes about the world of *haute cuisine* and the world in general. Kristin was utterly captivated by him. And he with her. In fact after two or three glasses of champagne they began to get a little more captivated with each other than I cared for. So I simply 'wanted' him to return to his normal unintelligible way of speaking again and once Kristin couldn't understand what the fuck he was talking about things reverted to the *status quo*.

We spent the night at *Le Manoir* and the following day set off on the long drive to the West of Scotland. I've always enjoyed driving, Kristin was excellent company and we chatted about this and that for most of the journey. During a rare lull in the conversation she suggested we had a little music on the stereo and asked what I'd like to listen to.

"You choose," I said.

"Let's see what you've got here," she said, opening the CD storage compartment. "Do you have any Whitney Houston? I love Whitney Houston."

I smiled to myself. There was about as much chance of finding a Whitney Houston disc in my CD storage compartment as there was of finding a Great White shark. I would have preferred a Great White shark to be in there just so long as it didn't sing like Whitney Houston.

*

It was the landlord at The Grim Jogger who had mentioned that I wasn't the only man who couldn't bear the sound of Whitney Houston's voice. There'd been something about it in the newspaper. It was the frequency of her voice that was the problem. It had the same effect on his dog; it set it off howling even worse than Whitney Houston. I remember feeling sorry for the dog; at least men could switch off Whitney Houston when she suddenly came on the radio unexpectedly.

Music had also gone through a major upheaval in my heaven. Whitney Houston was one the first casualties, given the boot unmercifully, never to assault my eardrums again. She'd been quickly followed by Leona Lewis and all other women who screamed rather than sang. Men followed; Jamie Cullum, the singer who specialises in singing standards not as well as the singer who originally performed them, had got up my nose for the last time; James Blunt had been blunted; Luther Vandross had sung the last of his dross. And Bono had been got shot of again, just in case I'd forgot him the first time.

All Rap and Hip-Hop music had perished.

Rap had plagued me from the moment I first heard it. I absolutely hated it. My favourite group is the Beatles. Great music, great lyrics, and you can hear every one of the words. The Stones and Dylan follow close behind. Great music again, although with Jagger and Dylan you can't always make out the words. But that doesn't matter, the tune is more than good enough to carry it. *Honky Tonk Woman? A Hard Rain's Going to Fall?* What's not to like? But rap? Rap is a double whammy. There isn't any sound in it that can remotely be called music, nor can you understand any of the words, save for the occasional one or two, and those are more likely to be 'Fuck yo bitch' than 'Michelle, my belle'. Words you can't hear properly, no music. What's to like?

Of course no one has to listen to rap music. But sometimes you have no option, it's with you before you know it; in films, on television, on the radio, in pubs, blaring out at about a hundred and twenty decibels from passing cars with their windows wound down, and all chanted by 'artists' who hide behind aliases such as Ice Cube and probably others with names like something you keep in the fridge, Lo Fat Spread and Mole D Cheese, for all I know.

I banished almost all present day musical offerings. Music may not have died when Don Maclean sang that it did in *American Pie*, with the death of Buddy Holly, but it was in the musical equivalent of the cancer ward by the time the 1980s arrived. So all boy bands had gone. Along with all girl bands. Coldplay, obviously. All male singers who sang in high voices. Plus everyone who has won X-Factor. And Bono again, just to make absolutely sure that I'd never again be subjected to the pontificating prat's views on global warming or whatever other of the planet's maladies he was currently going on about instead of just getting on with the singing.

Nowadays, if I was accidentally exposed to music from a passing car or a hotel bar, it was always by something I liked to listen to, the aforementioned Beatles, Stones and Dylan, The Eagles, The Kinks. Heaven.

*

Now, failing to find any Whitney Houston to expose me to, Kristin exposed me to The Arcade Fire, one of the few modern day bands, along with The Killers, to avoid my axe. It put a smile on my face.

So did the West of Scotland . It was exactly as I imagined it would be. But then it couldn't be anything else; I wanted it to be wonderful so it was wonderful: Even Middlesbrough or Rotherham would be wonderful if that was what I wanted, although I had no intention of visiting either to confirm it. Death is too short.

After a lovely week in Scotland we flew to America. Quite frankly I was a bit disappointed with it. Nothing wrong with the country, I expected a lot from it and it was everything I expected. But that was the problem; for having seen its skyscrapered cities, it's drive-in movies, its diners and its motels in countless Hollywood movies, along with its small-town life and endless countryside and deserts, it felt as if I'd already been there, as though I were making a return visit, not visiting it for the first time.

We started the trip in New York but after two days in the Big Apple I gave it the Big E. Too big, too busy, people in too much of a hurry, no time for anyone, just like I found London to be the only time I visited it.

Driving up through New York State to the Niagara Falls was much more to my liking. Much of it is Red Indian country, or had been when Red Indians populated it a century earlier. Many of the towns have Indian names; Ithaca, Susquehanna, Cayuga. I made Kristin laugh by suggesting it might not have been a bad idea if the Indians had called their settlements name s like Fuckoffwhiteman or Pissoffcuster, names which might have discouraged the people who eventually drove them from their homelands.

Hundreds and hundreds of square miles of the state is heavily wooded. Happily it now stands every chance of remaining heavily wooded, inasmuch as the world's need for wood pulp is concerned, thanks to my purge on books.

*

I love books but hate padding in books, whole passages put there by the author with no more ambition than a desire to bolster the word count; sentences, paragraphs, sometimes whole chapters that could easily be discarded without losing one iota of the story. All works of fiction in my heaven now contain no padding whatsoever. Every vestige of it has been removed. All that remains in a book is the story. The average novel has been reduced from three hundred and fifty pages to a hundred and ten. Books previously up to three inches thick are now three quarters of an inch thick at the very most. A book as thick as a brick would now need to have a brick in it. Several of Stephen King's novels (Stephen King of Padding), are now less than half an inch thick, all but one of them less than a hundred pages. All books are much better for it.

A week later I removed all smut. Having already had the padding removed from them every book ever written by Jackie Collins all but disappeared. As did Jackie Collins, along with Joan Collins, when I turned my attention away from books and onto all people who had undergone cosmetic surgery.

*

Kristin had seen the Niagara Falls before; she'd once appeared in a film that had been shot nearby. On the way there she said that the Niagara Falls is something else. I made her laugh again by asking her what was it then, the Victoria Falls? When I saw the Falls I had to agree with her, it is something else, something special. Before my purge on padding there would now be a long paragraph, probably three pages long, describing in great detail millions of gallons of the majestic Niagara River crashing, tumbling, cascading downwards before crashing on the stark, jagged rocks two hundred feet or more below. But not now.

We thoroughly enjoyed our visit to Niagara. We would have enjoyed it even more if the whole area hadn't been populated by Americans dressed in Bermuda shorts the size of Bermuda.

"Americans aren't like this in the films," I said. "They're all slim and good-looking with about twice as many teeth as anyone else. I don't see many of those around."

"I think it was Daniel Day Lewis who said that they must keep them all in a big warehouse in Hollywood and bring them out only when they have a film to make."

"Daniel Day Lewis could well be right." I have a lot of respect for the star of *The Last of the Mohicans* and many other classy films. In addition to being a splendid actor Daniel Day Lewis is the male equivalent of an English Rose. Especially as he has three names.

We had skipped breakfast and feeling hungry after our visit to the Falls we called in at nearby branch of Friendly's. I remembered Friendly's diners from one of the many road movies I've seen over the years. Kevin Bacon was in it as I recall. He ordered bacon and I remember wondering at the time if it had been put in the script especially, maybe for a joke because he was called Bacon, and if in the original script his order had been for eggs, Americans seemingly always ordering eggs for breakfast.

Our waitress had the customary American politeness and gave us a big welcoming smile, displaying the usual quota of brilliant white teeth. (I have always felt that Americans have more teeth than other human beings. Being exposed to them over the last few days confirmed this. Maybe they need the extra teeth to bite their way through all the food they have to consume in order to eat themselves into the gross state many of them are in?) When I ordered breakfast and the waitress asked how we'd like our eggs I returned her smile, though not with as many teeth, and displaying my knowledge of American road movies and breakfast habits said, "Sunny side up."

"You got it," replied the waitress, in the way all Americans tell people they've got it before they've got it.

Our intention was to stay in the area one more day, doing the usual touristy things, driving around, stopping off here to see a waterfall here, a picturesque ravine there, whatever took our fancy. The following day, before our planned drive back to New York, and having enjoyed our breakfast at Friendly's, we returned for another. We sat in the same place so we got the same waitress. She put on the teeth show again, and pencil poised over notebook asked if she could take our order. Kristin asked for scrambled eggs. I went for bacon and eggs.

The waitress refreshed her smile, and obviously remembering me from the day before said brightly, "Sunny side up?"

"Over easy," I said, once again displaying my knowledge of how Americans have their fried eggs.

"You got it."

She was about to go and get it when I had an idea. I said to her, "Do you work every day?"

" 'cepting Friday. Every day from opening through 'til two, for my sins."

It was Wednesday so she'd be on tomorrow. "We have to stay another day," I said to Kristin immediately the waitress

126

had left with our order.

"What about New York?"

"No we've got to stay."

"But we're due to fly back from Kennedy early Thursday morning. I thought you wanted to see New Jersey, where *The Sopranos* was filmed?"

"It can wait. This will be even better. "

"Why will it?"

"Did you see *Five Easy Pieces*, Jack Nicholson?"

"Yes, it was excellent."

"You remember the grief the waitress gave him in the diner?"

Kristin fixed me with a look of reproof. "You're not going to start arguing with the waitress are you?"

I crossed my heart. "Promise."

"What are you going to do then?"

"You'll see."

The following morning we went back in Friendly's. Same welcoming smile from the waitress. Same teeth show. Kristin ordered blueberry pancakes. I ordered bacon and eggs again.

"And how would you like your eggs this morning, sir, sunny side up or over easy?" said the waitress.

"Over hard."

"Eggs over *hard*?" She frowned. "Ain't never heard of *that* one before."

Kristin put a hand to her mouth, suppressing a giggle.

I feigned helpfulness. "I think its eggs over easy but you let them fry a bit longer."

"You have eggs over hard in the Yookay?"

"All over the Yookay. Our transport cafes can't do them any other way."

"Noo one on me. I'll have a word with Chuck the griddle chef, see what he can rustle up."

She headed for the kitchen, shaking her head, muttering, "Eggs over *hard*?"

Kristin elbowed me in the ribs. "You *are* awful, Norman."

I flashed her a grin. "Good though, wasn't it."

"Hilarious."

Something struck me. "Hey I wonder if there's a chain of diners called Unfriendly's? You wait for over an hour to get served and when you eventually get to give the waitress your order she tells you to fuck off?"

This made Kristin laugh out loud. "You really are a very funny guy, Norman."

"Well I can be."

"No, you have me in stitches sometimes, you really do. You should have been a comedian."

I paused reflectively for a moment, dragging back the past, before saying, "I thought about it once."

"Really? So what's stopping you? After all you don't do anything else." Immediately the words were out she looked apologetic. "Sorry, that came out wrong. I wasn't implying that you're the idle rich."

"That's all right." (When Kristin had asked me what I did for a living, soon after we met, she'd caught me unawares. The National Lotto had rescued me. A triple roll-over. Eleven and a half million. How an unemployed wages clerk or even a soon-to-be-employed plumber could have enjoyed my lifestyle would have taken a bit of explaining.)

"It would give you an interest," Kristin went on. "A purpose. A person needs a purpose in life."

I was reminded that The Archangel Phil had said exactly

the same thing. Man's need of a job. The next day I gave it some thought. Maybe they were right. My time in heaven had been and still was wonderful but there was no doubt about it that each week it was getting just that little bit less wonderful than it had been the week before, despite my taking the precaution of having a bad day about once a fortnight. But if I were to have a purpose it would have to be something other than being a stand-up comedian. Once bitten and that. I would no more be able to bear an audience not laughing at my jokes in heaven than I had on earth. Then it dawned on me. That wasn't the case anymore. The audience *would* laugh. If I wanted them to.

CHAPTER FOURTEEN

"Good luck, Darling." In the wings of the Manchester Evening News Arena Kristin squeezed my hand.

I just about managed a smile. "Thanks."

She frowned. "You're sweating."

"Nerves."

"Don't be silly; what on earth have you to be nervous about?"

"They might not like me."

She took out a handkerchief and dabbed my temple. "Nonsense, they'll love you. You've wowed them every night, why should tonight be any different?"

I couldn't tell her.

It was the last night of a seven-night engagement I was playing at the MEN. The first six nights I'd gone down like a storm. As good as any stand-up comedian who had ever appeared there. As good as Peter Kay had the couple of times I'd seen him at the MEN when I'd been on earth.

*

The previous six nights had been marvellous. Everything had gone just as how I imagined it would. Half-a-dozen No Piss performances. Although I wouldn't mind betting a few in the audience had wet themselves laughing. Wave upon wave of laughter flowing over me. Twenty thousand punters in the palm of my hands, hanging on to my every word, their sides aching from laughing out loud. And at the end of the show stamping their feet and shouting 'More' until I allowed myself to be persuaded by their pleas, bounced back onto the stage and gave them more. And then more laughter, more cheers.

After, there'd been crowds outside, hanging around to catch a closer glimpse of me, to cheer me on my way, to touch me, shake my hand, slap my back, ask me for my autograph. "Sign this for me would you please, Norman? Put 'To Michelle' would you?"

"How do you spell that?"

"M....I....C...."

"No, 'to', how do you spell 'to'? "

This brought more laughs. "Did you hear that? What's he like?"

"He just never let's up, does he."

"He's as good as Peter Kay any day of the week."

"Better."

"He's shit hot is Norman, shit hot."

*

And I had been shit hot. But tonight it all might be different. It *would* be different, it *was* different. For tonight I wouldn't be 'wanting' the audience to like me. Tonight I would be letting them make up their own minds whether or not I was funny.

It was something I had to do. After all I had nothing to lose; if it all started to go pear-shaped, if the audience didn't laugh, I could always revert to wanting them to laugh, and they would laugh. But I wanted them to laugh because *they* wanted to laugh, not because *I* wanted them to laugh.

Six weeks had passed since the idea came to me.

*

The day after Kristin and I got back from America I'd wasted no time in checking out Manchester's comedy club scene. Apart from The Frog and Bucket, the pub in which I'd made an abortive attempt to try out at when I was on earth, there were four others, plus another at nearby Bury. All had occasional open-mike nights, nights where anyone could go along and try their hand at stand-up comedy. Over the next three weeks I tried my hand at all of them, some of them twice, nine performances in all.

For the first five shows I wanted the audiences to like me, which of course they did. On the sixth I let them make up their own minds. Swelled with the confidence my handful of performances had given me it had gone quite well. Not as good as when I'd wanted the audience to like me, but appreciably better than anyone else who'd been trying out that night. So good in fact that at one of the venues the manager offered me a booking. I didn't take it; I had bigger fish to fry.

On my next appearance, when I again allowed the punters to make up their own mind, it was different.

It was a slow night, there were less than forty people in the audience at the hundred-seater venue and ten of those were fellow would-be comedians awaiting their turn to put their necks on the block. At least two of them were drunk - not would-be comedians I hasten to add - and had given the previous occupant of the stage a hard time. I was no more than a minute into my routine when one of them shouted out "I've heard it before." His mate followed this up with "So have I; tell us one we haven't heard you sad bastard."

They hadn't heard the joke before, I was sure of that, it was my own material. Unless they'd heard it at one of the other venues I'd appeared at over the last week or two, and if that was the case what did they expect? Even so it threw me. I managed to carry on but it wasn't the same; the audience was smaller and less responsive than on my last appearance there, which didn't help. At one point, towards the end, nobody laughed at one of my jokes. Not a soul. Total silence. I felt like walking off the stage. I almost did. Instead, I wanted them to like me, and of course they did, even the drunks. The following night it was back to normal, I let the audience make up its own mind again and I went down well again. The same the following night, my last night of trying out at the comedy clubs. I then judged that I was ready and the following day booked the Manchester Evening News Arena for a week.

*

"And now will you please give a very warm welcome to....Norrrrrrrrrman Smith!"

"That's you," smiled Kristin. She gave me a quick hug and pushed me gently towards the stage. "Break a leg."

I felt more like breaking into a gallop. But not towards the stage, towards the exit and right out of the arena. However I somehow manage to get a grip of myself and walked slowly towards the centre of the stage. The applause from the audience as I stepped into the spotlight was deafening. The Manchester Evening News review of my opening night had been lavish in its praise, many of them would have read it, those who hadn't had maybe been told about it, about me; all of them were expecting something special.

I looked out into the sea of faces. Peter Kay was sat in the front row. I'd wanted him to be. I picked up the hand mike, tapped it in the time-honoured manner to check it was functioning properly, looked out into the audience, steeled myself, and went into my routine:

Are there any Muslims in the audience tonight?

I shielded my eyes with my hand, scanned the audience

and pretended to home in on someone.

Yes, you sir. Is that your wife with you? What do you mean you've no idea, she's wearing a burka?

The audience roared with laughter. I breathed a huge sigh of relief. Same opening gag as on the previous six nights, same audience reaction. One gag down, two hundred to go. Would the others go down as well? I'd find out soon enough. I took a deep breath.

And talking about women who wear burkas how about the one who was up in court for making herself into a human bomb? Her parents said they were going to stand by her. But not too close.

Another gale force of audience laughter hit me. It was going well. It was going to be all right.

The judge let her off. She went BOOM!

The audience went wild. Peter Kay was laughing as much as anyone. I got into my stride.

But wearing a burka? I mean what's that all about?

"I believe you've got a new girlfriend, Sarfraz?"

"Right."

"What's she like?"

"She's got lovely eyes."

"What's the rest of her face like?"

"I don't know, I've never seen it, she always wears a burka".

"Has she got nice tits?"

"Who knows?"

"I won't ask if she's got a fanny."

Well how would he know, all the clothes they wear? When they have one of these arranged marriages many a time the groom never sets eyes on the bride until the wedding day. Even if it's not an arranged marriage all he's seen of her before is her eyes. He could always ask her what she looks like I suppose. Oh yes? I mean she's going to tell him she's got a face like the back of a bus, isn't she?

"What do you look like, love?"

"Shite".

I don't think so. She could tell him she looked like Catherine Zeta Jones with a body like Rachel Hunter but she could look like Andrew Lloyd Webber with a body like Keyhole Kate for all he knows. Imagine the first night of the honeymoon. She removes her burka....

"You've got a moustache!"

"Hasn't that Smooth Appeal Wax got rid of it all?"

"It would take a lawnmower to get rid of that lot. And I hope that tattoo will come off."

"It's not a tattoo it's a birthmark."

"Birthmark?"

"My mother was frightened by a dog."

"She wasn't frightened love she was bloody terrified. Have you seen the size of it!"

"My dad says it's shaped like Pakistan."

"It's a big as bloody Pakistan."

Then she takes her clothes off.

"I thought you said you had nice legs?"

"What's wrong with them?"

"What's wrong with them? You've only got one. The other one's artificial."

"You can't see it normally."

"I can see it now. And why is it pink? You've got one brown leg and one pink one."

"They only do pink ones on the National Health."

"I'm not too keen on that hump either."

No, give me an English girl anytime; she might not be

perfect but at least you can see what you're getting. Mind you she doesn't stop like that for long....

Two hours later I left the stage to tumultuous applause. A star was born.

*

March 23rd. The NEC, Birmingham.

Why do dogs always smell each other's bums whenever they meet? I've heard of sniffer dogs but a dog's not going to find much in the way of drugs up another dog's bottom is it?

March 24th. The Hammersmith Odeon.

I mean all it will be able to smell after spending all day smelling other dogs' bums is shit. Give one a flower to sniff at. 'What's that Fido?' 'Shit'. Or an orange. 'Shit again.'

March 25th The Kelvin Hall, Glasgow.

Or a Big Mac. 'That's shit too'. Mind you it could be right there...."

The swiftly-arranged countrywide one-hundred night tour started the following day. It couldn't have gone better. I had the time of my life after death. There was only one bad night, Liverpool Empire, and even then it had only been bad because I'd wanted it to be bad, because I didn't want any scousers enjoying themselves. It was my bad day, and a bad day for them too, so hard luck.

The revues were marvellous. *'Brilliant new stand-up'* - Manchester Evening News. *'Never laughed so much in my life'* - Daily Mirror. *'Loved the gag about big tits'* - The Sun.

I was over the moon. In addition to having my heaven just as I wanted it I now had a purpose. I would be in 'heaven' and heaven forever. There was not even the remotest chance of me going back to earth. It was all just wonderful. There was only one way in which it could be more wonderful.

CHAPTER FIFTEEN

Robert de Niro suddenly turned sideways on, cocked an imaginary hand gun and pointed it at me. "Are you talking to me? Are *you* talking to me? Are you talking to *me*? Well who the hell else do you think you're talking to? Well I'm the only one here....you talking to me? Who the fuck do you think you're talking to?"

It was all I could do to keep from giving my hero a round of applause. Instead I offered an apology. "I didn't really like asking," I said. "I mean people must ask you to do it all the time."

He nodded. "They do. And I usually tell them to go fuck themselves. But hey, it's your wedding day, Norman. If a man can't be indulged on his wedding day when can he be indulged?"

"Are you talking to me?" I replied, in a fair impression of de Niro's *Travis Bickle* character. "Are *you* talking to me? Who the fuck do you think you're talking to?"

De Niro fell about.

Bobby was to be best man at my wedding. The usher is Jack Nicholson - I'd already had Jack smash through the bathroom door with an axe, leer at me with crazed eyes and say 'Heeeeere's Johnny'. The groomsmen are Al Pacino, Ben Kingsley and James Gandolfini. I had toyed with the idea of having them appear in character, Pacino as *Scarface*, Kingsley as *Don Logan* in 'Sexy Beast' and Gandolfini as *Tony Soprano* but shelved it in case they frightened the wedding guests.

Helena Bonham Carter is matron of honour. Seven of the eight bridesmaids are English Roses. The eighth, for a laugh, is Sue from Stockport. I just saw her arrive. She has a broken nose now.

Four hundred guests will be attending the wedding ceremony, to be held at Westminster Abbey. Elton John will sing 'Norman's English Rose', with specially written lyrics to the tune of 'Candle in the Wind'.

Norman's English Rose
Though she'd never heard of him at all
He wanted her
And now they're one
He'd loved her from afar
But now his time for really wanting her has gone
Or I'm not Elton John....

(When I'd approached Bernie Taupin to write the lyrics he'd been indisposed so Elton had been forced to write the lyrics himself.)

A reception will follow at the Savoy Hotel. The catering is in the very capable hands of Raymond Blanc, assisted by Michel Roux and Gordon Ramsey. (As part of the entertainment, for me at least, wedding guest Graham Norton - allowed back for one night only - will ask for a bottle of Heinz tomato ketchup to shake onto Ramsey's langoustine and spinach terrine and the scatological chef will emerge from the kitchen, call Norton a stupid little Irish twat and crack him one over the head with a soup ladle.)

The music will be provided by The Beatles. Paul McCartney has promised not to play anything he's written since The Beatles split up, especially *The Frog Chorus* and

Mull of Kintyre. (A few weeks after The Beatles had got back together again they'd played at my fifty- third birthday party. The Fab Four had all seemed completely at ease with each other again, although Lennon, mischievous as ever, had almost spoiled it all by suggesting that Paul McCartney's marriage to Heather Mills had broken down because he'd composed a song in her honour entitled *I Want to Hold Your Leg*.)

Chris Tarrant will compere the cabaret. Ten seconds after he's kicked off the evening illusionist David Copperfield will make him disappear, my having unaccountably failed to get rid of him during my original purges. Two seconds later Derren Brown will make David Copperfield disappear, for the same reason, and take over the compering duties.

Comedy will be in the capable hands of Peter Kay. He will be very, very funny, but not as funny as me. Support will be Victoria Wood singing *Let's Do It* and John Cleese and Michael Palin performing *The Parrot Sketch,* joined immediately afterwards by the rest of the Python's for a rousing rendition of *The Lumberjack Song.*

Following the reception Kristin and I will leave for our honeymoon to an undisclosed destination.

Originally we were going to have a fairly low key wedding. Just a few close friends of Kristin's and a few friends I'd made during the six months I'd been in heaven, the Sir Alex Fergusons, the Wayne Rooneys, the Michael Caines, The Archangel Phils. I didn't want a fuss and Kristin wasn't bothered either way. But in the way I can never make up my mind who is my favourite actor, Robert de Niro or Jack Nicholson, I hadn't been able to make up my mind which of them to have as my best man. In the end I'd plumped for de Niro, but as I also very much wanted

Nicholson to be there too and didn't want him to feel he'd been left out of things I asked him to be the usher. Then Kristin suggested it might be a nice idea if all the groomsmen were my favourite actors too. I thought it a great idea. Then I'd come up with the idea of the Elton John thing and before we knew it we had a full-scale wedding on our hands. It didn't bother me; big wedding or small at the end of the day I would have Kristin as my wife.

*

Resisting the temptation to get my best man to do the *Rupert Pupkin* stand-up routine from *The King of Comedy*, one of my favourite film sequences of all time, I excused myself. The nuptials were only an hour away. Time to dress for the big day.

CHAPTER SIXTEEN

I knotted my shot silk grey cravat and checked my appearance in the mirror. The mirrors were very classy at the Savoy, gilt-edged, just like my future.

I had a deeply satisfied smile etched on my face. It said to me 'Whoever would have thought this would happen, eh? Humble little Norman Smith from Harpurhey, Manchester, getting married to the famous film star and English Rose *par excellence* Kristin Scott Thomas? Well he was. And in less than half-an-hour. So put that in your pipe and smoke it.

I took a few moments to reflect on my good fortune. I recalled what I was just six short months ago, the rough time I'd had of it during the preceding six months, the not much better time I'd had of it before that, the many years after my dad had died and I'd been lumbered with my mother. I compared it to the future I had in front of me with my beloved Kristin. I really, but really, was in heaven.

Kristin and I had never discussed children. I had never imagined myself as a father. I scarcely imagined I would ever get married; it had never been more than a hope at best. But things were different now and I rather liked the idea of a little Norman or a little Kristin. Or maybe a little Norman *and* a little Kristin? I was thinking about this, thinking I might bring it up with Kristin after the honeymoon - not before, I didn't want her going all mumsy on me when making love would be the main item on the agenda - when the door suddenly opened. It was The Archangel Phil.

I was both surprised and delighted. "Phil! You managed

to make it after all."

The Archangel Phil had been one of the first names on our wedding list but unfortunately he'd had to cry off at the last minute due to work commitments - an airplane carrying twenty three Roman Catholic priests had crashed with no survivors and six of them were on their way to heaven. Phil had to meet and greet them.

"No. No it's something else," The Archangel Phil said. "Something's come up."

"Oh?"

He didn't answer right away. I began to worry; I didn't like the apprehensive look on his face or the way he kept shifting his weight from one foot to the other. Finally he said, "I'm afraid there's been a bit of a hitch."

A bit of a hitch? What did he mean, a bit of a hitch? It suddenly hit me. Kristin! She'd had second thoughts. My stomach did a somersault. I tasted bile. "Is it Kristin?" I gasped out. "She hasn't changed her mind, has she? Please don't tell me she's changed her mind, Phil."

"No. Not that."

I breathed a huge sigh of relief. As long as it wasn't that I didn't care what it was. I smiled and said, "What then?"

"You have to go back."

"What?" I thought he meant to Manchester. "Back north you mean? Why?"

"No, to earth. You have to go back to earth."

"To earth?"

"You shouldn't be here. It was another Norman Smith who should have come to heaven."

"Another Norman Smith?"

"He was in the next ward to you at the hospital. Another cancer victim. It was he who should have died. There was a

143

mix-up and...." The Archangel Phil shrugged and spread his hands in a gesture of apology. "It does happen occasionally I'm afraid. I'm sorry, Norman."

I was completely thrown. Completely at a loss. "But....I don't want to go back."

"Yes I realise that, but the other Norman Smith is waiting to come but he can't until you've been safely returned."

"But....I mean I love it here, Phil. I love Kristin. I'm getting married. I'm getting married to Kristin, we're getting married in half-an-hour."

"I'm sorry Norman, truly I am, but there's just nothing I can do about it."

I was utterly devastated. My mind raced. What to do? A straw appeared from somewhere. I clutched it. "Let him stay. This other Norman Smith. Let this other Norman Smith stay on earth and I'll stay here. I'm sure he'd rather do that, nobody wants to die." This made perfect sense to me and I was convinced The Archangel Phil would go for it. I breathed more easily and forced a smile. "There, that's settled."

But The Archangel Phil's face told me it wasn't. He said, "I'm afraid that's not possible, Norman. Apart from that the other Norman Smith is in a very bad way. Such bad way that he wants to die."

"*I* want to die," I said. "*I* want to be dead, Phil. Besides, I'm already dead. I died on the operating table. You told me."

"That was my information. But apparently you get better, you respond to the new treatment, your cancer goes into remission and you make a complete recovery."

I became desperate and started to rant. "I don't *want* to make a complete recovery. I don't *want* my cancer to go into remission. I want to be *here*. I want to be here, with Kristin. I want to be here in heaven and getting married to Kristin."

The Archangel Phil stepped forward and put a comforting arm round my shoulder.

I clasped my hands together and looked up in anguish. "Oh God, please let me stay and get married to Kristin. Please let me stay. " I wasn't appealing to God when I said this, I was saying "Oh God, please...." in the way people on earth say it when they're faced with something they can't handle. The Archangel Phil didn't realise this and said, "God knows all about it, Norman. There's nothing he can do about it either. But I'm sure he'll watch over you."

That only made things worse. "Watch over me? Watch over me? Well I hope he makes a better fucking job of it than he did the last time." I pushed The Archangel Phil away from me and stuck out my chin. "Well I'm not going."

"You must, Norman."

Another straw appeared. The final one as it turned out. "All right. But after the wedding, after we're married. Let me get married first." I was sure he'd go for this. And after the wedding I'd think of something, we'd run off somewhere, hide, live in a cave somewhere, anything. But he didn't.

"I'm afraid it must be immediately."

"No!"

"Let go of that trouser press."

In a panic I'd grabbed the first thing that might anchor me in heaven, the wall-mounted trousers press. The Archangel Phil took a step towards me.

"Keep away from me Phil," I shouted. "I'm not going. And you can't make me."

"I'm afraid I can, Norman."

145

I suddenly felt a great force pulling at me. My feet lifted off the floor. I clung on desperately to the trousers press. In a shower of splintered wood and plaster it tore from the wall.

PART THREE

BACK TO EARTH

CHAPTER SEVENTEEN

As the train pulled out of Piccadilly station I picked up the freebie *Metro* someone had left on the seat opposite and settled back with it. Normally I like to look out of the window on train journeys but I'd travelled on the same line a week previously and was aware that the first part of the journey from Manchester to New Mills, passing through the city's drab and dingy eastern suburbs, is better spent with your nose in a newspaper, or even in the air, than pressed to the window. A Tesco plastic bag, selected by the slipstream of the train from amongst the sundry detritus decorating the tracks, momentarily attached itself to the window, reminded me of this, as though I needed reminding. Only when the train has negotiated Stockport, a town where trees are looked upon as tourists, does the terrain give way to more pleasant surroundings, and by the time you've reached New Mills, eight or so miles further up the track, you are in open countryside with wonderful views of the Pennine Chain's Kinder Scout. It was the first of two journeys I took that day that would end much better than they started. Or so I thought, for a short while.

*

There had been no sense of passing through a tunnel on my return to Earth. One minute I had been protesting to The

Archangel Phil that I didn't want to go back, the next minute I was back in Ward 12. Dr Who doesn't travel faster.

My first thought on coming round was that it had all been a dream. As I looked around Nurse Baker bustled by. I called to her and asked what day it was.

"Oh you've come round at last," she said with a smile. "Welcome back to the land of the living. November the tenth, all day."

"What time?"

She checked the upside down watch on her uniform. "Ten past two."

"AM or PM?"

"PM."

The same day I'd had the operation. Just three hours had passed since I'd gone down to the theatre. So it must have been a dream.

"And do you mind telling me what that thing is?" Nurse Baker said.

"What thing?"

"That!" She nodded in the direction of the wall beside my bed.

Propped against the wall was the trousers press that had come away from the wall of my room at the Savoy in heaven. "Only you were hanging on to it like grim death when you came back from the operating theatre; it took two of us to prise it out of your hands."

I smiled weakly and shrugged. "Search me."

Not a dream then. But then how could it have been? It would have taken a lot longer than three hours to dream of all the things that had happened to me while I was in heaven. And I could remember every last second it. All my time with Kristin, all our love-making, all Manchester United's victories over Liverpool, all the meals at Michael Caine's *Abode*, the trip to Niagara Falls, Friendly's, *The Sopranos*, every joke in every performance of my career as a stand-up comedian, the wedding plans, Robert de Niro, the aborted wedding, everything, and all in glorious Technicolor and Stereophonic Sound. But time, as The Archangel Phil had explained to me, was timeless in heaven, so it all must have taken place during the three hours I'd been under the anaesthetic or coming round from it.

And now I had the cancer ward to look forward to again. I was back in the overcooked cabbage and stale pee smelling giant tropical fucking fish tank again with a colostomy bag strapped to me for the rest of my life.

My hand had gone to my diaphragm to check if the dreaded colostomy bag was back in place the moment the trousers press confirmed to me that I hadn't been dreaming. "Shit," I said, appropriately enough, when my fingers touched its clammy plastic.

There is nothing, but nothing, in the entire world, worse than having to wear a colostomy bag. For me at least. I've always been squeamish about shit; any wife of mine would have been on her own at babies' nappy changing time if I'd ever married, English Rose or no. It's the one reason I've never owned a dog, even though I'd have loved one. But having to put its shit in a little plastic bag every time I took it out for a walk then spend the rest of the walk carrying it as if it were the shopping was too high a price. And now I had a plastic bag of my own shit to carry around with me every time I went for a walk. At least the dog shit carriers could hang their plastic bag of shit on a tree and collect it on the way back from their walk then throw it in the wheelie bin when they arrived home. I couldn't even do that.

I once read somewhere that some deaf people develop an unconscious dislike of their hearing-aids and often punish the offending apparatus by allowing its batteries to run down. This got me to wondering how I could exact revenge on my colostomy bag. Making a hole in it so it couldn't do its job properly was one of the ideas I came up with. Simply not emptying it until it eventually burst was another. But as both methods of retribution would result in me being covered in my own shit, the first sooner, the second later, but more spectacularly, common sense had prevailed.

But at least I hadn't got cancer any more, according to The Archangel Phil, or wouldn't have when the chemotherapy and radiotherapy and whatever other therapy they'd got lined up for me - shit-scaring therapy probably - had done its vicious work, which was something to be thankful for. Dr Matthews confirmed this three weeks later. My cancer had gone into remission. Chemotherapy would ensure it stayed in remission. It had been a miracle. I had been very, very lucky.

"Lucky? Oh yes, I'm lucky all right," I replied to this, in a voice that implied exactly the opposite.

Dr Matthews had been unable to understand why I wasn't absolutely delighted with the news, and said as much. I could have told him that a course of chemotherapy followed by living in Harpurhey for the rest of my life with a colostomy bag strapped to me, after having spent the last six months colostomy bag-free shacked up with Kristin Scott Thomas, was not conducive to a feeling of absolute delight. I hadn't bothered in case he suspected I was losing my marbles and had me moved to the psychiatric wing. Stranger things have happened in National Health hospitals.

Dr Matthews told me that I was probably still suffering

from post-operation depression and that I'd soon snap out of it. I knew otherwise; it was post-heaven depression that ailed me and it would take a lot more than a snap to get me out of it, nothing less than major seismic activity would suffice.

A positively beaming Reverend Ever told me that my recovery was a miracle. The Lord's work. But not entirely unexpected, in fact not unexpected at all, as he had prayed for me. While the Reverend Ever was rejoicing I recalled telling The Archangel Phil that I owed the cleric an apology. He didn't get one. He was unbearable enough as it was, telling all the other patients how his prayers had saved me and that as he'd also prayed for them it was only a matter of time before they too made a complete recovery. This had the effect of perking up the other eight patients no end, but they all perked back down again two days later when Mr Gearing, throat, breathed his last. (Three months later, when I was back at 12 Hugh Gaitskill Street, The Jehovah's Witnesses didn't get an apology from me either. When next they knocked on my door I remembered what would be happening to them when they eventually made it to heaven - that they'd very soon be on their way back - and it was all I could do to keep my face straight, let alone apologise. In fact it was the nearest I'd got to a laughing since returning to Earth.)

Mr Gearing's demise prompted Mr Meakin to say that he had gone to a better place and Mr Broadhurst to go along with this viewpoint. Mr Braithwaite, Mr Statham and Mr Greening nodded in agreement. Mr Hussein also nodded, but as he had his earphones on he was probably nodding, not to the beat of Meatloaf this time, but to The Kings of Leon, as Mr Fairbrother had mischievously suggested to him that as a vegetarian it was perhaps a bit untoward of him to listen to a band with meat in its name, and Mr Hussein, seeing the error of his ways, had gone along with it.

At that point I entered the conversation. In the feeling of utter despair that had filled my waking hours since finding myself back on earth, not to mention the chemotherapy, which if anything was even more vicious than the last lot I'd had, I had completely forgotten to tell the rest of the patients in Ward 12 how wonderful it was in heaven.

"He'll be a lot better off in heaven," I called out to them. "A whole lot better. It's an even better place than you imagine."

Mr Meakin's head snapped round. "I thought you didn't believe in God? Changed our minds now he's cured our cancer, have we?"

"One of us now, is he," said Mr Broadhurst, with a self-satisfied smile.

I took my time before replying. I couldn't very well tell them I'd been to heaven and returned to earth; they were all believers but even they wouldn't believe that. After a moment I said, "I'm a believer myself now. God spoke to me."

"Go on?" said Mr Greening in disbelief.

"What did he say?" said Mr Braithwaite.

"He told me I'd be a lot better off in heaven."

"Really?" said Mr Meakin, and added, in case his query should indicate an element of doubt in his belief of the powers of the Almighty to communicate with his subjects, "Well I can't say I'm surprised. It doesn't surprise me in the least."

"Yes, God said it's quite wonderful up there," I went on. "Everything a man could hope for."

"Did he say you get the legover?" said Mr Fairbrother,

revisiting an old concern.

I gave a smile of fond memory. "Not only do you get the legover," I said, and delayed the rest of the sentence a moment for effect, "but you get to have it with anyone you want."

"Fuck me!" said Mr Statham.

"Anyone you want?" said Mr Braithwaite.

"Anyone," I reiterated.

Mr Fairbrother didn't even need to think about it "I'm going to have it with Cameron Diaz," he said, licking his lips at the prospect. "Three times a day."

Mr Braithwaite's eyes widened. "Three times a day?"

"I was always a three times a day man," said Mr Fairbrother.

"If I had sex with Cameron Diaz three times in a day it would kill me," said Mr Greening.

"Then you might be better off having sex with someone you'd like to have it with, but not more than once a day, Mr Greening" advised Mr Broadhurst. He thought for a moment. "Someone like Dot Cotton perhaps."

"Oh I could manage Dot Cotton more than once," said Mr Braithwaite, "I quite like Dot Cotton."

"Emily Bishop then."

"It doesn't matter who you have sex with and how many times you have it, it can't kill you," I said, before Mr Braithwaite had the chance to tell everyone how many times a day he'd like to shag Emily Bishop. "You're already dead. That's one of the best things about heaven - because you're already dead you can't die again. Being dead is quite wonderful. According to God," I added quickly, as it was beginning to sound a bit like it was coming from me. "In fact if you all want to do yourself a favour the very best thing you could do is stop taking your chemotherapy."

"Stop taking our chemotherapy?" said Mr Fairbrother, as though I'd suggested he stop breathing. "Chemo is the only thing that's keeping me alive."

"What do you want to keep yourself alive for when you can be in heaven getting your end away with Cameron Diaz?" I said.

"And Dot Cotton," added Mr Broadhurst.

In the meantime Mr Meakin had become suspicious. "I notice that you yourself are having chemotherapy, Mr Smith."

I gave a deep sigh. "I can't think why."

And I couldn't. And before it eventually dawned on me that by subjecting myself to the chemotherapy that would complete my remission it was too late, it had already cured me.

*

I'd never been to New Mills before, although I'd been quite near to it the previous week on my visit to Lyme Park, Disley, a mile or so distant, just over the border with Cheshire.

When I got off the train I made straight for the town's main tourist attraction, The Torrs Riverside Park. I'd read about it in a brochure I'd picked up at Lyme Park; it looked well worth a visit and if I was going to do something that might help to 'take me out of myself', as Auntie Betty constantly advised me I needed to do, as good a place as anywhere to visit. I knew there was little chance of it taking me out of myself but it would please her that I was doing it, that I was seen to be making an attempt - Auntie Betty had been wonderful to me while I'd been in hospital and afterwards, so it was the least I could do.

The park, just a short walk from the railway station, is quite something, I was to discover. But much better than that. It held the answer to all my problems.

*

I had gone to Lyme Park the week before because Kristin was on film location there. They were filming a medieval comedy, *Middle Ages Spread.* Auntie Betty had mentioned it when I'd been round at her house the day before; she'd read about it in the evening paper. Apparently they were filming a crowd scene and needed hundreds of extras. She suggested it might be a good idea to go along, I liked films, it might be fun, I liked a laugh, or I used to before I got all miserable. It might have been fun at one time, but not now. She might just as well have suggested I stared at the wallpaper for an hour. Which was more or less what I'd been doing for the last hour, when I hadn't been staring at the floor. In an effort to tempt me she told me how nice it was at Lyme Park, she and Uncle Reg at been there once, there was a stately home and herds of deer and a visitor centre, so even if for some reason I didn't get a job as an extra I would have quite a nice time there. "The BBC used it when they were filming *Pride and Prejudice,*" she enthused. "It's where Darcy met Elizabeth Bennet."

"Good for Darcy," I replied, totally disinterested.

"But you might get to meet someone famous," Auntie Betty persisted. "You never know. Sean Connery is in it, you like Sean Connery. And who was that other one they mentioned was in it, that comic, you like him, now what was his name....?" She checked in the newspaper. "Peter Kay. Peter Kay's in it. All sorts of famous film stars are in it according to this; Judy Dench, Jo Brand, she's that one off the telly isn't she - Kristin Scott Thomas....I've never heard

155

of her...."

I had. It brought me bolt upright in my chair. "Kristin Scott Thomas?"

"Yes, have you heard of her?"

Had I heard of her? I nodded.

"You ought to go then, it might help to take you out of yourself."

I needed no further invitation, taking me out of myself didn't even enter into it; it was an opportunity to see Kristin again.

Auntie Betty and Uncle Reg, bless them, hadn't known what had got into me. I'd been discharged from hospital for over a month, it was almost four months since I'd had the operation, two months since I'd completed the chemotherapy, and to all intents and purposes I'd made a complete recovery. But no one would have known it. I didn't behave like a man who had virtually been given another life. I just didn't want to do anything. Nothing. Every time Auntie Betty called on me, which was often as she worried about me, she found me sat in an armchair moping, and if I wasn't sat in an armchair moping it was because I was still in bed moping. I never went out, I was smoking heavily and drinking even more heavily, evidenced by all the empty beer and wine bottles in the overflowing wheelie bin in the back garden. "All that smoking, you'll be getting cancer again if you're not careful," she admonished me.

"Good."

"You ought to get out of the house and get a bit of exercise, you'll be seizing up."

"Good."

"And you shouldn't be drinking as much as you are either, you'll make yourself ill."

"Good."

She shook her head. "You'll smoke and drink yourself to death, you see if you don't."

"Good."

I hadn't thought of that benefit and started smoking and drinking even more.

In an effort to get me out of the house for even the hundred yards or so that separated our homes Auntie Betty encouraged me to visit she and Uncle Reg more often, "So you won't just sit here feeling sorry for yourself - although why a man cured of cancer should feel sorry for himself I really have no idea," but this only resulted in me sitting in their house moping. "I don't know what ails you, Norman," she said. "I really don't." I did. I wanted to die. I had my life back but I didn't want it back, I wanted to be in heaven with Kristin.

Well I might not be in heaven with Kristin, I reflected, on arriving at Lyme Park a week later, but it will be heaven seeing her again.

I was fairly confident I would see her, even though it might be from a distance, as according to the newspaper all the principals would be taking part in the crowd scene. They were filming a large country fair with its various attractions, sideshows and jugglers and fire-eaters and strolling minstrels and whatever else constituted a country fair in the Middle Ages. Everyone would be there, the complete pecking order, the Lord and Lady of the Manor, their heirs, their servants, smallholders on their land, cottagers, freemen, gamekeepers, peasants and serfs. Kristin, I had found out, was Avrill, the eldest daughter of the Lord of the Manor. Norman Smith, I found out when I arrived at the film set along with a thousand other people hoping to be extras, would be a serf, the lowest in the pecking order. I wasn't surprised; I was just glad to get safely through the audition.

At first I had toyed with the idea of telling the PA that I'd had previous experience as a serf, in the hope that I might be chosen as head serf, if there is such a thing, or maybe given a speaking part - we were talking here of a man who had appeared in *The Sopranos* and *The Wire* - but in the end decided against it as it would only draw attention to myself, the last thing I wanted if I were to get within touching distance of Kristin.

In fact getting through the audition, such as it was, was a piece of cake. If you could breathe you were in. The only two who didn't make it were a man wearing bottle-bottom glasses and another wearing a large National Health hearing-aid, both of whom were told they wouldn't be required as their aids to failing senses were anachronistic for a film set in 1540, even if it was a comedy. A man with an aluminium Zimmer frame, initially rejected on the same grounds, but more of an opportunist than the other two, was taken on after he suggested that as it was a comedy his Zimmer frame might go down well with the audience, especially if the film's carpenter knocked him up a wooden one.

The chosen serfs, about two hundred of us in all, were taken to a large marquee to be fitted out with our costumes.

I was kitted out like the rest of them in a selection of what the film's costume designer had decided was the attire of a typical serf in the Middle Ages; blouses made out of a rough sacking-like cloth, fastened at the waist with a leather belt or piece of rope, coats of a thick woollen material which fell from the shoulder to halfway down the legs, leggings of various shades of brown, and boots. There weren't enough boots to go round but those without boots were told by the

PA, winging it I suspect, that there weren't enough boots to go round in mediaeval times either, so they'd look the part. All the clothes were the same size but all the serfs weren't, so most of them fitted where they touched. When one of the serfs complained the PA told him that serfs' clothes were always ill-fitting and asked him where he thought he was, Matalan? The serf said no, nothing fitted him at Matalan either, which got a laugh and made everyone feel a bit better about the way they looked. I didn't care what I looked like; they could have dressed me up as Coco the Clown or sent me out buck naked with a feather duster stuck up my behind just as long as I got the chance to see Kristin again.

When we'd finished dressing and the PA was happy with us, a state of affairs in inverse proportion to the degree the serfs were happy with their costumes, a team of make-up girls descended on us and made us look even more like serf-like by dirtying our faces with a greasy mud-like substance and decorating us with a variety of facial blemishes. I watched apprehensively as the serf next to me - an accountant from Wilmslow he had mentioned to the serf on his other side, a fat town councillor from Chapel-en-le Frith (a possible ancestor?) - was adorned with the ravages of smallpox and two boils, which he seemed quite happy about. Although I got away with just a large wart on the end of my nose I was much less happy as naturally I wanted to look my best for my meeting with Kristin and the wart didn't do me any favours. Rather than complain about it in the hope they'd let me remove it, which I was pretty sure they wouldn't if the man who had objected to his hump and smallpox was anything to go by - all that his grumbling brought him was a bit more smallpox for his cheek and for his cheek - I decided I would remove the offending wart

159

when the time came that I met my love, provided it hadn't been stuck on too hard.

When the chief make-up artist was happy the assistant director, an intense, flustered-looking young man with a cockney accent, told us what each of us would be doing and what was expected of us. I was to be a spectator at a cockfight and would be expected to look interested. I asked him, hopefully, and as casually as I could, if Kristin Scott Thomas would be attending the cockfight. He looked at me suspiciously then warned everyone that they must stay where they'd been put and not go roaming off anywhere, he didn't want any of them wandering about star-spotting - when they were shooting *Black Death* one of the extras had walked up to Sean Bean as he lay bleeding to death after four horses had torn him in half and asked him for his autograph and he didn't want any of that sort of thing happening today, thank you very much; everyone was to remain in their allotted area until told to move somewhere else.

In the event Kristin was about a hundred yards away from the cockfight, seated on a raised dais with what I took to be her parents, watching a jousting competition. I could just about recognise her. She looked lovely, even from that distance, or I imagined she did. She would have looked lovely from the Moon.

Peter Kay turned out to be one of the cock fighters. He passed within touching distance of me - our eyes met briefly - as he made his way, stroking a cockerel, through the crowd encircling the cock pit. A buzz of excitement and a smattering of applause and laughter welcomed him. "What are you laughing at, I'm only stroking me cock." he said, looking aggrieved, to more and bigger laughs.

Once the fight had got under way and everyone was

wrapped up in the action I detached myself from the rear of the spectators and joined the serfs who had been detailed to aimlessly mill around. My milling was more aimed and five minutes later found me about thirty yards away from the dais, and Kristin. Between us was a roped off area where the jousting competition was taking place. At the moment there was a break in the proceedings while they were re-setting the scene so I took the opportunity to duck under the rope and into the jousting area.Trying to look as nonchalant as possible I started to make my way across the space between us. I hadn't gone more than five yards when there was a sudden shout of "Action!" quickly followed by the thudding sound of hooves. Startled, I looked to my left to see a knight on horseback bearing down on me. A second later came an enraged bellow of 'Cut!' In a panic, I retained just enough composure to realise that I was in a lot more trouble than just a knight with a lance heading for me and that if I didn't act pretty smartly it was the nearest I was going to get to Kristin, so instead of turning back I continued in the direction of dais. There was an angry shout of "For fuck's sake get that twat off my set!" and three of the film crew ducked under the ropes and made to head me off. By then I was only about fifteen yards away from Kristin, who had turned to see what all the fuss was about. Our eyes met. It stopped me dead in my tracks. I raised an arm in the air, waved to her and called, "Kristin, it's me, it's me, Norman." She looked at me blankly and shrugged, puzzled. It was the last thing I saw of her as at the same moment one of the film crew grabbed hold of me. He was quickly joined by the other two, and together they hauled me bodily from the jousting field.

The assistant director who had briefed the serfs was waiting for us, spitting feathers. "What the fucking hell do you think you're playing at?" he bawled at me. "Do you realise how much it costs to set up a shot?"

I couldn't have cared less.

"Get him off the set," he went on. "Pay him off and boot him out. No. Don't pay him. Just boot him out."

Two of the film crew frog-marched me back to the tent where I'd donned my serf costume and told me to change and sharp about it then get the hell out of it if I knew what was good for me.

What would have been good for me would be another chance to see Kristin. But how could would that be possible after what had happened? With the benefit of hindsight I would have gone about things differently, more cautiously. I certainly wouldn't have been fool enough to wave and shout out "Kristin, it's me." I don't know why I did it in the first place, she wouldn't know me no more than Peter Kay had known me when we'd briefly made eye content at the cockfight; this was earth not heaven, neither of them would have known me from Adam.

"Right, now clear off out of it." said one the film crew men, when I'd finished changing.

I thought that if I could just hang around for a bit longer I might be able to come up with something. I could smell bacon cooking and it gave me an idea. "Could I have something to eat?" I asked. "I haven't had anything since breakfast and I'm starving; they said there'd be bacon barmcakes and coffee."

"That's for people who behave themselves," said the man. "So on your way."

He made to manhandle me again. I don't know where it came from, desperation I suppose - I've always found that fanciful lies come easily to me when my back is against the wall - but I suddenly said, "Look, I'm diabetic, if I don't get something to eat pretty soon I'll go into a fit. You don't want that on your conscience do you?"

The man looked me up and down and turned to his mate. "What do you think?"

"I foam at the mouth," I added, and loaded the trowel. "It's horrible." Then laid it on thick. "I could very well swallow my tongue and turn blue."

The other crew man shrugged but looked concerned nevertheless. His mate shouldered the responsibility. "Go on then. And then clear off. If I see you you're in deep shit."

I smiled my gratitude. "Just as soon as I've had my bacon barmcake. And thanks."

When we emerged from the tent one of the men pointed to a marquee about fifty yards away. "Grub's there." He needn't have bothered; the wonderful smell of bacon cooking travels a lot farther than fifty yards. Thankfully, or I would never have had the idea.

I thanked them again and set off in the direction of the marquee. Then, with a look over my shoulder to check they weren't watching me, carried on right past it. Earlier I'd noticed the park's cafeteria-cum-visitor centre some hundred yards or so farther on. A cup of tea would be welcome while I figured out a plan of action.

There were quite a few customers in the cafe, people who had come along to watch the day's filming in the hope of catching a glimpse of their favourite stars. After buying a mug of tea at the self-service counter I found a seat in a quiet corner. Someone had left a brochure on the table. It told of other attractions in the vicinity of Lyme Park. One of them, it turned out, was The Torrs Riverside Park. I put it in my pocket to read later on the train then set about thinking what

I might do to get close to Kristin again. After ten minutes or so I gave it up as a bad job. It was hopeless, I was in normal clothes now, I'd stand out like a sore thumb, so what chance was there of getting anywhere remotely near her? No chance. Besides, I consoled myself, I'd seen her once already, I'd done what I set out to do, if I saw her again it would only be the same. So after I'd drunk my tea I left Lyme Park and headed for the station.

*

The Torrs Riverside Park, the 'park under the town' as it is styled, is set in the bottom of a deep gorge gouged out of the hard sandstone during the ice age (so a notice displayed in the heritage centre later informed me) and situated at the confluence of the rivers Goyt and Sett. It is 'under the town' insofar as towering ninety feet above it are two high-level road bridges connecting the three different areas of the town which looks down on it, just two of many bridges, road, river and rail, contained within the gorge. The park itself is most attractive, with its old mill ruins, weirs, aqueducts, disused chimney stacks, cobbled tracks, low-level stone arched bridges scattered here and there, and the elegant if incongruous *Millenium Walkway* metal aerial bridge that winds its way through the gorge, clinging precariously to a massive retaining wall, atop of which is the Manchester/Sheffield railway line. A further feature seemingly out of time and kilter with its setting is a large Archimedes screw Hydro-electric generating system. An information board informed me that kingfishers and dippers could be seen on the park's two rivers, but if so they were having a day off. (Careful Norman, this is getting very close to padding. Enough said.) Despite the absence of the promised bird life, there was enough of interest in the park to remove my misery for a while. But it was back, like a great black cloud, soon afterwards.

*

Three months after returning to Earth, a month after being discharged from hospital, I had started work with Bob Hill, Plumber. My first job was less than auspicious - a blocked WC. "We get a lot of that," my employer informed me, information that I, with my dislike of shit, could have done without. Sanitary towels were the cause of the blockage. "It's usually when they have young girls in the house," Bob said knowledgably, obviously an authority on the subject. "Their mothers warn them not to put them down the lavvy but they take no notice." Far too much information already but more was to come. "But hairdressers are the worst, hairdressers' shops. I think the customers save them for when they have their hair done. I go to one place at least once a month; I'm surprised I'm not invited to their Christmas party. 'Hair Today' it's called. They ought to call it 'Sanitary Towel Today'."

There were two more blocked lavatories that week. One on Tuesday, the other on Wednesday. The one on Tuesday was sanitary towels again, the one on Wednesday a teddy bear that a toddler had decided need a bath. It resurfaced from its short stay down the u-bend with a sanitary towel wrapped diagonally over one eye, giving it the appearance of *Children in Need's* Pudsey Bear. And it was covered in shit of course. Pudsey Bear in Need. In need of a good scrubbing. I heaved when I saw it. There were no blocked lavatories on Thursday otherwise I might not have lasted until Friday.

Even if my future hadn't contained a seemingly constant stream of lavatories to unblock - and Bob Hill said the week's tally was 'about normal for the time of the year'. (Did it vary from summer to winter? Were there more lavatories to unblock in spring and less in the Autumn? I didn't ask, I didn't want to know.) Even if it had all been fitting central heating boilers and radiators and plumbing-in washing machines, even if friendly housewives had plied me constantly with tea and biscuits as I went about my work, even if the providers of tea and biscuits had been English Roses and offered me sex along with the Typhoo and chocolate digestives I would have jacked it in after the first week. I just couldn't cope with it. It wasn't just the plumbing and the shit; I wouldn't have been able to cope with any job. The memories of my time in heaven were too strong. The wonderful, marvellous time I'd had there, especially the times with Kristin, were in my thoughts every minute of my waking hours, and many of my nocturnal ones too; I just couldn't get them out of my head no matter how hard I tried, no matter how much I tried to ignore them.

"You've got to give yourself a bit of time, lad," said Bob Hill, when I told him I was quitting. "You've had a rough time of it by all accounts."

Little did Bob Hill know that I'd had exactly the opposite of a rough time, and that it had given me a taste for the good things in life that even the most successful plumber would never be able to afford in his wildest dreams. How many new bathrooms would you have to fit to earn enough money for Manchester United to win five-nil every week? How many central heating systems would you have to install to tempt Kristin Scott Thomas into your bed? On a more realistic level, how many new washing machines would you have to plumb in to earn what a top stand-up comic makes?

It was this last thought that prompted me to thank Bob

for his sympathy but that my mind was made up. I wondered why I hadn't thought of it before. The following day I phoned each of Manchester's comedy clubs to find out when their next open-mike nights were.

*

A sign pointed the way the town's heritage centre. Having had enough of the park and feeling all my troubles boil to the surface again I took the short but stiff climb up out of the gorge to see what the centre had to offer. It just might grab my interest and temporarily lift my gloom for a bit.

The walls were covered in information boards detailing the various developments in the town's history, along with old photographs and posters – *'Town Hall. Dance to Jimmy Armstrong and his Band. 1s/6d. Jiving or Be-Bop are Prohibited'*; *'The New Mills Brass Band, Est. 1812, will perform a Grand Victory Concert'*; *'1912 May Queen Celebrations in the park, floats, fancy dress, visiting Queens, All Welcome'*. There was a coal mine tunnel, a reminder of the thirty pits the town once had, and tables and shelves containing old ledgers and books documenting the town's history from its start as a farming community through its rapid growth and transition into a mill town - hence New Mills - during the Industrial Revolution, to its present function as a dormitory town for Stockport and Manchester. Pride of place was taken by a large model of the town as it was a hundred and fifty years ago with all the cotton mills, long since demolished, still standing. I noted that the high level bridge crossing the River Sett had already been built and a second bridge, that would be known as the Union Road Bridge, over the River Goyt, was still under construction. While I was looking at the model a man came over and spoke to me. I had been just about to leave but what the man said made me change my mind. And my future.

I left the heritage centre then. To look down into the park under the town from the bridges above it. Before returning home.

*

The manager at the Frog and Bucket didn't recognise me of course. Nor did the two would-be comedians who had been trying their luck the night I'd been doing likewise. It seemed strange because then the manager had been all over me with offers of work, and one of the two comedians had buttonholed me and asked me for tips. Well maybe the manager would offer me some work tonight, there was no reason why he shouldn't, I had the material, I had the technique - we were talking here about a stand-up who had completed a sell-out one hundred night countrywide tour.

It was a good night, the place almost full. Despite my track record I was nervous. I couldn't 'want' the audience to like me, but I hadn't done that when I was in heaven, both in the comedy clubs, eventually, and later on tour. I would be fine, I was sure, despite the nerves. Any butterflies in the stomach would disappear once I was out there, once I'd got my first laugh. And there were no drunks in the audience, I noted with relief, no one to shout out "Tell us one we haven't heard you sad bastard."

The first two acts had gone down well, which was a further gratifying sign. And neither of them had been anything special - if the audience found them funny they'd find me hilarious. The third bloke wasn't funny at all. Like most of the comedians who try out at comedy clubs his humour was in observation; the problem was he hadn't observed very much. "Am I the only person in the world who wonders why the Queen always looks to the left on coins and looks to the right on stamps?" he asked the yawning audience. Well yes, probably you are, everyone else has better things to do with their time than gawp at stamps and coins to see which way the Queen happens to be looking. And that had been it. That was all the observation the observational comedian had observed; that the Queen always looks to the left on coins and looks to the right on stamps. He had no answer to this strange phenomenon, no amusing suggestions as to how it might have come about. That maybe Her Majesty looked to the left on coins because when she'd sat for the photo the photographer had told her it was her best side but when she'd sat for the stamp Prince Philip had blacked her left eye the night before.

So, having been bored rigid by observations about the Queen's head and which way it was looking on different units of exchange, and similar gems – by far the best of which was "My wife's into *Feng Shui*, she keeps moving the furniture round for optimum happiness. She moved the wardrobe last night but it doesn't look any happier to me" - the audience were in less than good humour when the fourth act up that night, me, took the stage.

It went wrong from the start. "*Are there any Muslims in the audience tonight?*" The problem was that there weren't. If there had been it all might have turned out differently.

When I'd appeared at large arena venues I'd looked far into the audience and addressed a 'pretend' Muslim with the follow-up line of "*Yes, you sir. Is that your wife with you? What do you mean, you've no idea, she's wearing a burka?*" But when you look out into the audience at the Frog and Bucket - miniscule by comparison - you look directly at someone; there's no alternative. And with no Muslims in the audience - and no wives present even if there had been a

Muslim - I'd had to look at someone. Unfortunately the man must have been a member of the British National Party - or at the very least in sympathy with its ideals - as he immediately sprang to his feet and said in a threatening manner, "Who the fuck are you calling a Muslim you fucking arsehole?"

It threw me completely. It would have thrown Peter Kay. "Sorry. I wasn't meaning....sorry."

"Well just fucking watch it, twat."

"I've said I'm sorry. It's just that...."

"Oh get on with it," came a raucous voice from the back.

Pulling myself together I tried to do just that. *"And talking about women who wear burkas how about the one who was up in court for making herself into a human bomb? Her parents said they were going to stick with her...."* I realised my mistake the moment the words came out of my mouth and tried desperately to get back on course. *"Stand by her. Her parents said they were going to stand by her."*

But it was too late. The tag had been blown. I didn't bother with another joke. I walked off the stage and straight out of the Frog and Bucket without stopping. I didn't try again.

*

I crossed the first of the high level bridges, the Union Road bridge, and walked on to the second, the Queen's bridge. The man who came up to me at the heritage centre had said, indicating the Queen's bridge on the model of the town, "You see that bridge. Bloke chucked himself off it last week."

It was of course the answer to all my problems and I'd realised it immediately. I couldn't think why I hadn't thought of it before. Suicide. Jump off the bridge and

170

seconds later I would be dead and back with Kristin.

When I arrived at the Queen's bridge I didn't pause for even a second. Looking quickly to left and right to see if anyone was watching - there wasn't but it wouldn't have made any difference if there had been - I took a grip of the top of the iron railing, vaulted over it and plunged ninety feet to my certain death.

When I hit the shallow water of the river I didn't stop; I entered a tunnel, this time pitch black, and kept on falling.

PART FOUR

IN HELL

CHAPTER EIGHTEEN

I fell a further few feet beyond the end of the tunnel and landed flat on my back with a sickening thud. Every breath of air was knocked out of my body. I screwed my eyes tight shut in pain. My hands felt the ground beneath me. It was solid, hard to the touch. Had I missed the wooden bench in Piccadilly Gardens and landed on the pavement? Or maybe I wasn't in Piccadilly Gardens, where I expected I'd arrive, maybe I was somewhere else, maybe I was still in New Mills, in New Mills heaven?

No matter, all that was important was that I was back where I belonged; if I did happen to be in New Mills I could soon get the train back to Manchester, and from there on to Lymm, and Kristin.

But wherever it was I'd ended up there was a heck of a racket going on. A large number of people were shouting excitedly, whistling, cheering, rebel-yelling. I forced my eyes open. The first thing I noticed was that I wasn't outside; there was a ceiling high above me. Suspended from its rafters were what looked to be spotlights and loudspeakers. And were those TV sets hanging in mid-air? *Where was this?* I struggled painfully to a sitting position and looked around. I gasped in amazement. I was on the set of a huge television studio. In front of me was the studio audience.

Behind me a huge television screen, sixty feet high or more, its screen split into nine sections in rows of three, like one side of a gigantic Rubik's Cube. The whole screen and each of its sections was bordered by strobe lighting which pulsed on and off every second, a different garish colour for every pulse. Giant mirrors at either side, the same size as the screen, reflected and multiplied its nine sections into twenty seven. A battery of laser beams criss-crossed the screen from corner to corner, top to bottom, side to side. Dry ice carpeted the floor. Simon Cowell would have had a an orgasm.

No sooner had I taken in the scene than a lantern-jawed presence with an artificial air and artificial hair minced towards me, stopped, leered down at me and said, "Nice to see you....to see you, nice. Welcome to hell. I'm your mentor. Your *tor*mentor. "

"Fuck me," I said.

"I will be doing, Norman, I will be. And at every opportunity," said Bruce Forsyth.

The audience erupted.

Bruce affected delighted surprise, turned to them and clapped his hands together. "What a wonderful welcome! Such a lovely audience. So much better than last week's."

The audience replaced the whooping and hollering with laughter and warm applause.

The object of their affection turned his cadaverous grin on me and said, "I bet you thought you'd be going to heaven, didn't you?" Then, with another trademark leer at the audience "The fool!"

The audience whooped and hollered and rebel-yelled even louder. Bruce encouraged them, arms outstretched, conducting them. Then, with a quick left to right sweep of his baton he silenced them instantly and said, "Tell Norman why he hasn't gone to heaven, ladies and gentlemen, boys and girls."

"Because he's committed a mortal sin," the audience chanted as one. Bruce nodded sagely in agreement. "Right. Because he's committed a mortal sin." He turned to me and cupped an ear. "What's that, Norman? You thought that was just for Catholics? Yes well you know what thought did, don't you. Followed a muck cart and thought it was wedding. But in your case he thought he was going to heaven and he was going to hell. So how do you like those apples?"

I didn't answer. I couldn't. I was literally struck dumb.

Bruce showed mock concern. "Aw. Cat got your tongue? I think Norman must be a bit shy ladies and gentlemen. Aw."

"Aw," echoed the audience, taking their cue.

Bruce turned his attention back to me. "Now where was I?" He thought for a moment then pretended to remember. "Ah yes." He took hold of my hand as if to help me to my feet but immediately let go of it with an expression of distaste. "Ooh! Ooh, you're all clammy. He's all clammy, ladies and gentlemen." He shook his head and tut-tutted. "Where have you *been*, Norman, you bad boy?" He shook his head in despair. "I don't know, I really don't. The things I have to do to make a living." He took hold of my hand again as if holding a dead rat would have been preferable, put it on my stomach, felt around for a moment and placed it on my colostomy bag. I grimaced as I was reminded of it. This drew another smirk from Bruce. "Yes, it's still there, Norman, this isn't heaven you're in now; this is a million miles from heaven." Then, with a grin at the admiring audience he said, "And now I've got a little surprise for you. Because you're my favourite. He's my favourite, ladies and

174

gentlemen." He moved my hand a few inches to the left. I caught my breath. "That's right, another colostomy bag, Norman. Your Brucie bonus. I know how much you like them."

The audience roared with laughter.

The voice-over clown from *Dancing on Ice* now added his two pennyworth. "Ooh he didn't like that!"

The audience went wild.

Bruce continued, by now at his oiliest. "But as you know, you get nothing for a pair...." He cued the audience.

They responded. "Not in this game!"

"So it's on with the show. And *what* a show we have for you tonight ladies and gentlemen, boys and girls, viewers at home."

At a signal from Bruce two stage hands carrying a hard-backed chair descended on me, hauled me bodily to my feet, dumped me on the chair, strapped me to it and span me round so that I was facing the huge television screen. Bruce turned to the audience and announced, "Let the entertainment begin."

To the biggest eruption of applause yet from the audience all nine sections of the television screen, augmented by their reflections in the giant mirrors, suddenly burst into life. I was completely engulfed in television screens. They were showing nine of my most hated programmes - A *Carry On* film; *Strictly Come Dancing; The X-Factor; Alan Carr, Chatty Man; Coronation Street; Britain's Got Talent*; Jonathan Ross presenting an awards show; *Loose Women;* and *I'm a Celebrity Get Me out of Here*. All in HD and Dolby Sound.

For the next three hours I was forced to watch them while the studio audience whooped and hollered and laughed and screamed and rebel-yelled and applauded. The only break in the proceedings was when a member of the audience, suspected of having an IQ of over 30, was dragged out screaming and replaced with Prince Andrew.

Every five minutes or so, for a few seconds, one of the programmes took on a starring role, zooming out of its section to fill the entire screen. The image of one of the perma-tanned uninformed nonentities who comprise the panel of the *X-Factor* suddenly became nine times larger and said to one of the totally untalented contestants, "You nailed it." A clip from the cunt and tit show *Coronation Street* - "So Steve cunt come then?" "In tit a shame." A scene from *Carry on Cleo* - "I'm sorry sir, but for the good of Rome you must die." "But you're my personal bodyguard and champion gladiator. I don't want to die. Treachery! Infamy! They've all got it in for me!"

The *Carry On* clip tipped me over the edge. I screwed my eyes tight shut to block it out - I couldn't do anything about having my ears assaulted by the programmes but I didn't have to look at them. Oh yes I did, because the moment my eyes closed an electric shock of such intensity it caused my head to snap back coursed through my entire body.

"Oh dear, he liked that even less than he liked the second colostomy bag!" said the *Dancing on Ice* voice- over.

"Wait until he realises there's another one on his back," joked Bruce.

The members of the audience stamped their feet and roared their approval, by now making more noise than a thousand children with attention deficit syndrome who had just had their Calpol confiscated.

Every so often one of the screens changed to another hated programme; re-runs of *Big Brother, Celebrity Stars in their Eyes, EastEnders*, the onslaught of pap was relentless.

I was absolutely bereft. Was this what it was going to be like forever more? Sat here watching Jonathan bloody Ross and Alan bleeding Carr and Loose fucking Women for all eternity? And it would be for all eternity; there could be no release from it because, as with heaven, I couldn't die because I was already dead. I consoled myself that at least it couldn't get worse. Bruce stepped forward.

"And now it's over to the football."

The nine sections of the screen merged into one.

"Manchester United versus Liverpool from Old Trafford." He turned to me. "Do you want to have a stab at guessing the score?"

CHAPTER NINETEEN

Hell isn't hot. There are no streams of fire, no smell of brimstone. Nor is it anything like any other description I've ever seen of hell. No hoofed demons with horns sticking out of their head, no smell of excrement, no raging inferno. What it is, I came to realise about halfway through my initial ordeal in front of the giant television screen, is the other side of the coin to heaven; a place where everyone has their own personal hell.

I had woken some time later in a room much like a prison cell with damp, bare stone walls and a stone-flagged floor. I had no idea how long I'd been there. The room was just about big enough to swing a cat in but only if the cat ducked as it went past the stone wash basin in the corner. The only other items in the room were a WC, a table and three chairs, and, high in a corner, a large loudspeaker. I was wondering why there were three chairs at the table when the cell was obviously for a sole occupant when the answer was suddenly provided for me, quite horribly, when the iron door swung open and Ant and Dec bounded in.

"Hello Norman mate," said Ant. "Welcome to *A Me-al with Ant and Dec*."

They were each carrying two plates covered with silver cloches.

"Grub's up," said Dec, as the gruesome twosome made their way to the table and set down the plates.

I buried my head in my hands. I have never been able to look at Ant and Dec without wanting to bang their heads together and now they were apparently to be my dining companions

"Tournedos Rossini, potatoes au gratin, asparagus and baby carrots tossed in bu-ah," said Dec, removing two of the cloches with a flourish.

"For us," said Ant.

"And for you....Bushtucker!" said Dec,

"A rat's arsehole on tow-ast," said Ant.

"Only joking," said Dec, before I could begin to contemplate what a rat's arsehole on toast must taste like, "You're having a Big Mac."

On balance I think I would have preferred the rat's arsehole, whatever it tasted like. My expression must have said as much because Ant said, "And you can pick your chin up off the flow-ah because tomorrow it gets worse."

"Tomorrow it's two Big Macs."

"Then the day after it's Kentucky Fried Chicken."

"Then Burger King Whopper."

"Then Southern Fried Chicken."

"Then Eastern Fried Chicken - that's Southern Fried Chicken fried by a Chinaman in case you was wonderin'."

"Then we start all over again with a Big Mac."

"Breakfast is the full monty....for Ant and me."

"And an Egg McMuffin for you."

They grinned their cheeky chappie grins and sat down at the table. Only hunger persuaded me to join them. I looked down at the Big Mac on its cardboard plate. Normally I wouldn't even have considered eating it but by now I was starving.

"Now don't let it go get co-ald, man" said Ant.

I eyed the Big Mac as a rabbi might regard a pork pie. Perhaps it might taste better cold? It couldn't taste worse

179

than it did hot. I settled for hot if only to get it over with. Gritting my teeth I picked it up, braced myself and bit into it. It tasted even worse than I remembered.

"Hmmm, this Tournedos Rossini is hittin' the spot," said Ant, chewing on a big lump of steak, the sauce dribbling down his chin.

I glared at him. "Do you have to make so much noise when you eat?"

"Wouldn't be doing our job if we didn't make a noise when we was eating, Norman."

"Instructions from Ow-ald Nick himself," added Dec. "It's on our list of things you dow-ant like."

I wondered if their list included eating with their mouths open, because the steak in Dec's mouth was going round like cement in a cement mixer. I asked him.

"Afraid it is, Norman mate," he said, renewing his efforts.

"Well actually we're not afraid, we're enjoyin' it," said Ant.

In case I should remind them of any other nasty eating habits they'd perhaps forgotten to include in their repertoire I set about the Big Mac. When our plates were empty Ant said, "And now we've got a surprise for you, Norman."

Dec lifted the cloche off the fourth plate, revealing a thick leather-bound book. Which was indeed a surprise as I'd assumed the plate would have our desserts on it, tiramisu for Ant and Dec, shit with sugar on for me.

"Us lads are going to read to you for an hour," said Dec.

"Every day," said Ant.

"*Harry Po-ah,*"

"*And the Philosopher's Stow-an.*"

My head tried to sink back into my body.

Soon after the advent of the publishing phenomenon of the century I had tried reading the first of the Harry Potter books. My mother had bought it after seeing TV presenter Richard Madeley recommending it on the now defunct *Richard and Judy* show. Apparently he said he'd thoroughly enjoyed reading about the exploits of the boy wizard. Forgetting completely that Richard Madeley is the man who walked out of Tesco's with half a trolley full of wine without paying for it, claiming he'd forgot, and therefore his opinion was that of a man whose grip on things was so tenuous he'd once overlooked the fact that he'd acquired a shed load of wine between removing it from the shelves and arriving at the checkout, and so was not perhaps the best person to judge the literary merits or otherwise of a book, I started to read it. The experience gave me no reason to read another Harry Potter book and several reasons why not to. After thirty pages I had failed to see what all the fuss was about and after fifty pages had concluded that there wasn't anything in it to have a fuss about. I couldn't for the life of me understand why adults were reading it, and with apparent enjoyment, and arrived at the conclusion that it must be for the same reason that some adults ate Big Macs with enjoyment, except that in this case it was their brains rather than their taste buds that weren't fully developed. I conjectured that they were probably one and the same people, and that perhaps one day J K Rowling would write a book with them in mind, *Harry Potter and the Reconstituted Beef Enigma*.

"I get Harry Potter every day I presume?" I said, as Dec opened the book, crossed his legs and settled back to read.

"Until we've read all seven."

"And then we start on Jeffrey Archer," said Ant.

An hour later Dec closed the book and he and Ant bid me goodnight and left "Until tomorrow at the same time". I let out a sigh of relief, although the experience hadn't been as bad as it might have been as after the first few minutes I'd simply shut down my ears. They were re-opened in no uncertain manner the moment Ant and Dec closed the door behind them when the silence was pierced by a hundred decibels of Whitney Houston bursting out of the loudspeakers.

"And I....ay....ay.... Will always love you.... oo....oo....Will always love you...."

I screamed and jammed my hands over my ears. It kept out maybe about ten of the decibels.

CHAPTER TWENTY

The Rank Organisation

Presents

CARRY ON CARRYING ON

Starring

Sid James
Kenneth Williams
Hattie Jacques
Charles Hawtrey
Barbara Windsor
Kenneth Connor
Bernard Bresslaw
Joan Sims
Several Other Hams
with

Norman Smith

as
Ivor Big 'un

LS of a Roman encampment, somewhere in England.

Cut to inside Julius Caesar's tent. <u>CAESAR</u> (Kenneth

Williams) is reclining on a couch. He is being hand-fed grapes by a buxom <u>HANDMAIDEN</u> (Barbara Windsor).

HANDMAIDEN:
(TEMPTINGLY FONDLING THE GRAPES) Could you manage another, Caesar?

CAESAR:
Yes but let's finish the grapes first.

A <u>CENTURION</u> (Charles Hawtrey) enters with <u>IVOR BIG 'UN</u> (Norman Smith), a messenger. CAESAR turns to the CENTURION.

CAESAR:
And who have we here?

IVOR BIG 'UN:
Ivor Big 'un, Caesar.

CAESAR:
Well I've nothing to be ashamed of myself.

HANDMAIDEN:
I'll vouch for that. (GIGGLES)

IVOR BIG 'UN:
Alias Hugh Jampton.

CAESAR:
So, what brings you here Ivor Big 'un alias Hugh Jampton?

IVOR BIG 'UN:
Alias E Normas Cock.

CAESAR:
I said what brings you here?

IVOR BIG 'UN:
Alias Willy....

CAESAR:
(IMPATIENTLY) Oh get on with it for God's sake, we'll be here all day at this rate.

IVOR BIG 'UN:
Whatever you say, Caesar. Do you know The Appian Way?

CAESAR:
No I don't think I've ever tried that.

It was my fourth day in hell and I was being forced to watch the third *Carry On* film in which I'd appeared. The first had been in the starring role of Limp Sid in *Carry on Impotence*. In the second I was Thrust Deeply in *Carry on Fucking* (I believe I'm up for a BAFTA for that one).

My life had settled into a steady routine. Every morning at eight, after my Egg McMuffin, I was marched to the television studio where I spent the next sixteen hours strapped to a chair watching the giant television screen. Then it was back to my cell for my evening meal with Ant and Dec followed by hour of Harry Potter. Then my lonely bed.

All the things I'd got rid of in creating my very own heaven were now being employed to create my very own hell. If I hadn't known it when I'd first been strapped to the chair and subjected to the delights of *Strictly Come Dancing* and *The X-Factor* I knew it soon afterwards when Liverpool started banging in goals for fun against Manchester United and beat them thirty-five nil.

On my seventh evening in hell, more in desperation than in hope, I asked Ant and Dec how long the treatment was likely to go on for.

"Well for eterna-ee man, for all eterna-ee, how long did you think?" Ant said.

I'd known the answer before I asked.

Later, in bed, for the second time in twelve months, I wept. The first time had been when I was going through the trauma of chemotherapy and facing death. This was worse. This time I didn't even have the release of death to look forward to. As in heaven, I was already dead.

After I cried myself out I began to reproach myself. Why oh why couldn't I have left things alone, settled for things as they were? I hadn't been enjoying myself on earth, in fact I'd been bloody miserable, but what I had now was purgatory. It *was* purgatory. And it was all my own fault, all of my own doing. I should have tried harder, not given in as easily; I should have tried to forget all about Kristin, not go looking for her; that had only made things worse. I would have forgotten all about her in time, or if I hadn't forgotten her altogether I'd have stopped thinking about her as much.

I should have gone back to the Frog and Bucket and given it another go at stand-up. So what if the audience hadn't laughed? They might have laughed the next time. And once they'd laughed I'd have been up and running, I'd have had a job, making a living doing something I liked doing. And even if they hadn't laughed, even if they'd never

186

laughed, it would have been a bloody sight better than what I'd ended up with. Anything would be better than hell.

There was that plumbing job. I never gave that a fair crack. All right so I'd got a shitty toilet to unblock now and then but it was nothing like the shit I was now being bombarded with all day every day.

This thought was going through my mind for the hundredth time when the loudspeaker suddenly exploded into life.

Nigga had the fuckin nerve to call me immature
Fuck you think I made odd future for?

Apart from the hour that Ant and Dec read Harry Potter to me music was played every single second I was in my cell, except for the hours between midnight and 6 am. During that time it came on twice, at random times, for a random period, and at an extra twenty decibels.

To wearin' fuckin' suits and make good decisions?
Fuck that nigga, Wolf Gang
Who the fuck invited Mr I Don't Give a Fuck
Who cries about his daddy in a blog 'cos his music sucks

The music was always either Whitney Houston singing *I Will Always Love You* or Tyler the Creator rapping *Sandwitches*, which if anything I hate even more than Whitney Houston singing *I Will Always Love You*, as judging from what I've heard from him all that Tyler the Creator creates is verbal diarrhoea.

Well, you fuckin' up, and truthfully I had enough

187

And fuck Rolling Papers, I'm a rebel, I'm ashin' blunts
Full of shit, like I ate that John
Come on kids, fuck that class and hit that bong

The only good thing about it, and the reason why I didn't hate it more than I already did, was that I could only make out about a quarter of the words; and even then I only knew them because I'd already heard them about a thousand times. But even if I'd been able to decipher *'ashin' blunts'* and *'hit that bong'* I wouldn't have understood them; I have no idea what a blunt is, much less how to ash one, and God knows what a bong is. But then, all of a sudden, things changed and I could hear every word.

And fuck you too Norman 'cos yo in Hell
Cos yo been bad and topped yo sel
Taint hot there like they say but who give a fuck
This nigga ain't there so he don't give a fuck
Just here on CD to taunt yo ass
With rap shite rap shite all day long

"Christ all fucking mighty!" I beat the pillow with my fists and screamed out in anguish. Now the Devil had Tyler the Creator creating lyrics with me in them! I jammed my hands over my ears and screamed out again, loud and long. The moment I stopped screaming the rapping ended and Ant and Dec bounded in.

"We've got a treat for you tonight, Norman," said Ant.

I didn't like the grin on his face. Not that that was anything new.

"A hot wor-ah bottle," said Dec

"What?"

"A hot... wor....ah.... bottle," said Ant.

He gave a lewd wink as a girl aged in her early twenties stepped into the cell. She was not unattractive, if a bit cheap-looking, and dressed in a short black leather skirt, black leather boots and a low cut top that revealed too much cleavage and that she wasn't wearing a bra. Dec introduced her with a sweep of his arm. "Ria."

"Rita," said the girl with a scowl. "It's Rita."

"That's what I said."

"We'll leave you and Ria to it then, Norm" said Ant, making for the door.

"Leave me to what?"

Ant made a circle with the finger and thumb of one hand, inserted the index finger of his other hand in it and moved it in and out a few times.

I shook my head. "No thanks."

Dec smiled. "You will though."

"Once the Devil has got into you," said Ant.

They went out, closing the cell door behind them. Rita looked at me with disinterest. After a moment she folded her arms, tapped her foot on the floor impatiently and said, "So how am I supposed to get on the bed while you're on it?"

I had no intention of letting her get on the bed and told her so.

"I'm not doing it stood up," she said, tossing her hair, "I've got a bad back; it gives me backache if I do it standing up."

"We're not doing it."

"You have to. Devil's orders."

"Bollocks to the Devil."

I turned my back on her, pulled the blanket over my head and tried to get to sleep. I'd no idea what the Devil's game

189

was but I wasn't about to play it. To have sex with this Rita woman might give me a little relief from my suffering but if things worked out par for the course she'd probably have VD or crabs or something equally nasty and I'd end up in an even more miserable state of being than I already was.

I heard her high heels on the stone flags click-clacking over to the bed and then she was lying down next to me under the blanket. "Hutch up a bit," she said, "I can't get in proper."

I sighed, long-suffering. She was more persistent than the Reverend Ever. I gave her the Reverend Ever treatment. "Fuck off and leave me alone."

Instead she put her arms around me and started to gently stroke my chest. I pushed her hand away roughly but she immediately put it back and continued stroking. I became aware of her thighs spooned into mine and the soft mounds of her breasts pressed hard against my back. I tried to shut it out of my mind but a moment later my whole body started to shake violently and then suddenly stiffened as what felt like a large red hot knife plunged into my body and pierced my heart. It was the Devil entering me, I know now. Seconds later my body relaxed, leaving only my penis stiff - satisfyingly stiff for a man with the Devil in him. Rita took hold of it, rubbed it a couple of times and said, "Ooh, who's a big boy then?"

I turned to face her.

"How do you want me?" she said. "I prefer it from behind."

I couldn't have cared less as long as I got into her and quick. "Whatever."

We climbed off the bed. She quickly took off her top and skirt - she wasn't wearing knickers - got on her hands and

190

knees on the edge of the bed, turned to face me and said, "Ready when you are, lover."

I moved up to her, cupped her shoulders in my hands and pulled her back as I pushed forward and entered her. I closed my eyes, as I'm in the habit of doing when I have sex. I began to fuck her and she started moaning as though she was enjoying it, all part of the act I supposed. I couldn't have cared less, I was enjoying it so nothing else mattered. In fact it was very nice, although not of course as nice as it was with Kristin. It wasn't as nice as it was with Rita a moment later, when, on feeling a sudden change in the texture of her shoulders, from smooth to hairy, I opened my eyes to discover I was fucking a goat.

I have never moved so fast in my life. I reached the opposite wall in about two seconds flat. Unable to advance any further I turned to face the goat, my back pressed hard against the wall, my arms spread wide, hands pushing against the stonework in a futile effort to move myself even further away from it.

The goat, possibly wondering why its enjoyment had suddenly been curtailed, and certainly not getting any signals from me which might suggest to it that I'd be renewing our acquaintance in the immediate future, looked at me with a look of disappointment in its rectangular, dilated eyes, and bleated.

I pulled myself together and thought what to do. A moment later my mind was made up for me and I instantly became myself again when just as quickly as he had entered me the Devil left me. Unfortunately the goat didn't. Accepting that our affair had come to an end it looked away from me and started eating the pillow. It made short work of it and was making inroads on the mattress when Ant and Dec returned, grinning from ear to ear.

"Sorry about that," said Ant.

"Yes you look like you are," I said.

"Well you have to laugh, haven't you," said Dec.

Ant shook his head and chuckled in admiration. "That Ow-ald Nick, eh? I do-an't know how he thinks 'em up."

"But we're glad he does," said Dec. "Anyway, to business. We've to tell you that you can go back if you want."

"Back? Back where?"

"Well earth of course."

"Earth?"

"If you're up for it, like."

It took a moment to take this in. "You're telling me I can return to Earth?"

Ant and Dec nodded.

"Reincarnation," said Ant.

"You come back as a can of evaporated milk," said Dec.

"Hey that's a good one that, I like that," said Ant.

"Got it off a Christmas cracker."

I smelled a rat. Was this another way of inflicting more suffering on me? Probably. I said, "This is a trick isn't it? To make me feel worse than I'm already feeling. You tell me I can return to earth and when I take you up on it you tell me you're only joking."

Ant looked shocked. "Would *we* do that?"

"Ant and Dec?" said Dec, equally affronted.

I decided to go along with it for the time being. What was there to lose? "What do I have to do?"

"Sell your sow-al to the Devil," said Dec.

"Sell my soul to the Devil?"

Dec nodded. "Yes, you're one of the lucky ones."

"Or one of the unlucky ones," said Ant."

"What's that supposed to mean?"

"Ow-ald Nick only lets the ones go back he thinks he can have a bit of fun with."

I though it over for a minute. What did Ant mean, have a bit of fun with? The Devil seemed to get his kicks out of making your life a misery so presumably he thought that if he sent you back to Earth you'd be even more miserable. But how could that be? How could I be any more miserable than I already was? How could anything be worse than being forced to watch sixteen hours of crap television all day, when I wasn't being forced to watch Manchester United lose against Liverpool - the score had been 77-0 yesterday - eating nothing but junk food, having my ears constantly assaulted by Whitney Houston and Tyler the Creator, Ant and Dec reading Harry Potter with Jeffrey Archer next up, two colostomy bags, and having sex with goats? It couldn't. If the Devil was going to get into me again, and if he'd done it once he was certainly going to do it again whenever he had a mind to, far better he did it on Earth than in Hell.

"Tell him I'll do it," I said.

"He'll know," said Ant.

*

In the middle of the night I awoke but this time it wasn't the sound of Whitney Houston or Tyler the Creator that roused me from my slumbers. My whole body was shaking violently again. I stiffened as I felt the red hot knife enter my body and pierce my heart again. I felt my hair actually stand on end. Sparks shot from my head and I could smell my hair burning. Then nothing.

PART FIVE

AUF DER ERDE

CHAPTER TWENTY ONE

I awoke with a start. I was slumped in a chair, as though I'd fallen asleep there. I looked around. I was in a large, opulent office. It registered with me. I was back! I had sold my soul to the Devil and the Devil had kept his part of the bargain and delivered me to earth. But where on earth? Not back to where I'd previously lived, surely; they didn't have offices of such magnificence in Harpurhey, certainly. Nor from where I'd left earth, New Mills, from what I'd seen of it.

My eyes took a quick inventory. I picked out a large green leather-topped desk, empty but for two telephones and a framed photograph. A large, high-backed chair behind the desk. A number of matching, smaller chairs against a wall. A highly-polished wooden floor dressed with expensive-looking rugs. A filing cabinet and a writing bureau against one of the wood-panelled walls. Two highly wrought multi-candled chandeliers suspended from the ornate corniced ceiling, their illumination not required at the moment as enough natural light was coming from the three large windows, each of them framed by elaborate brown velvet drapes. On the walls, one of which held a large floor-length gilt-framed mirror, were several paintings. One of them looked like a Monet. It was certainly a room I'd never been in before. Yet for some reason it seemed familiar.

I looked down at myself. I was wearing knee-high brown leather boots. Tucked into the tops were brown serge jodhpur-like trousers. Above them a military-style tunic, the same colour and material as the trousers, leather belt diagonally across it from shoulder to hip and round the waist. I put a hand to my cheek. It didn't feel familiar; it was different to my cheek, the skin was a different texture, smoother; sallow? I explored further. My nose felt different too, sharper, slightly bigger, and beneath it a small moustache. And why did my hair, always brushed back, now have a right parting and hang down over my forehead on one side. Puzzled, I got to my feet, went to the mirror and looked into it. My eyes were immediately drawn to the swastika armband on my upper left arm. *What was this?* Then I looked at my face.

"Fuck me, I'm Hitler!" I said, or would have had I not been struck dumb.

I reeled. Literally. *Adolf Hitler.* So this was the Devil's price for my soul! To be returned to earth, not as Norman Smith but as Hitler, the man whom I had detested from the moment I'd become aware of him, the only human being I had ever truly hated. Transfixed by the frightful sight in the mirror I asked myself how the Devil could have known this? But then why wouldn't he? He'd known about my dislike for Bruce Forsyth and *Carry On* films and rap music and all the other things he'd continually plagued me with all the time I'd been in hell, so why not Hitler?

I closed my eyes, opened them and looked again. Hitler was still there, scowling at me; not an optical illusion, as I'd hoped, not a figment of my imagination but flesh and bone, my flesh and bone. Yet....I didn't feel like Hitler. Or at least what I imagined Hitler must feel like, a man constantly at boiling point, ready to erupt anytime, forever teetering on the edge of insanity; I felt like me, Norman Smith, Mr Ordinary Joe. *What was the Devil's game?*

It now came to me where the room was. What it was. Adolf Hitler's study in his country retreat in the Obersalzberg of the Bavarian Alps near Berchtesgaden. Not far from Germany's border with Austria, the country of his birth. I'd seen it in photographs of the Wachenfeld/Berghof, the name by which the house was known.

I went to one of the windows and looked out. It was a bright summer's day. Undulating green countryside stretched into the distance as far as the eye could see; there was a pine forest and the Bavarian mountains beyond. How could such evil have emanated from such a beautiful spot?

I wondered at the date. I noticed a newspaper on one of the chairs and checked the top of the page. June 29, 1936. Three years and three months before the outbreak of the Second World War. I searched my memory. In March of that year Hitler had defied the Versailles and Locarno treaties by remilitarizing the Rhineland. I sat down and reflected on my position. Why was I here? In particular why was I here now? Was it the Devil's plan that I should preside over the war? Was it his idea of the 'bit of fun' that Ant and Dec said he liked to have with people who sold him their soul? I shuddered; if that was the case not only would I be overseeing the war and the wholesale carnage it brought with it, I would be the man ultimately responsible for the concentration camps and the systematic murder of millions of Jews, gipsies, political opponents, communists, cripples, homosexuals and anyone else who didn't fit the Aryan template or simply got in my way. It would be the nightmare to end all nightmares. But....that couldn't happen now, surely? *I* wouldn't do that. *Norman Smith* wouldn't be responsible for murdering millions of innocent people, men, women, children, and I was Norman Smith. I might not look like Norman Smith, I might look like Hitler, but I was most definitely Norman Smith inside. Otherwise why would I be thinking like Norman Smith? Had the Devil perhaps messed up, botched my return to earth in some way? Had he sent me back as Hitler on the outside but somehow mistakenly left me as Norman Smith on the inside? It was beginning to look like that. And if that was the case....well, hard cheese Devil, there wouldn't be a Second World War if I was in charge of things. There would never be an invasion of Poland by Germany, the last straw that triggered off the hostilities; Germany wouldn't be invading Czechoslovakia's Sudetenland - the Fatherland could forget about that too. I smiled at the prospect. I was going to enjoy myself as Hitler. Before I could think of further horrific events in history that wouldn't be happening now that Norman Smith was in charge of things there was a discreet tap on the door.

"Come in." I gave a start. I'd said the words 'Come in' in English but they'd come out in German, "Kommen Sie herein." What was all that about? I don't speak German, only the odd bit I'd picked up from my war books and from Herman the German back at Manchester Central Library; 'Kommen Sie herein' was one of the bits I'd learned so maybe, aware that I looked like Hitler, I'd said it subconsciously. The door eased open. A man, shoulders stooped in deference, stepped cautiously in, as though half-expecting to be castigated for setting foot in Hitler's office even though he'd been invited to. He said, almost whispered, "Herr Goebbels and Reichsfuhrer Himmler have arrived, mein Fuehrer." Except that he didn't say that. He said, "Herr Goebbels und Reichsfuhrer Himmler sind angekommen, mein Fuhrer." But I heard it in English. *What was going on?*

The man waited patiently while I considered the implications of his announcement. Josef Goebbels and Heinrich Himmler. The Reich Minister of Propaganda and the Head of the Waffen SS. What did they want with me? Some business or other, obviously, terrible business if I knew them, they certainly hadn't come to wish me happy birthday. After a few moments the man wrung his hands apologetically and said, quietly coaxing, "Herr Goebbels and Reichsfuhrer Himmler, Herr Hitler?"

I took a deep breath. There was nothing for it but to admit them. "Tell them I will see them now." But the words came out in German again, "Sagen Sie Ihnen, ich werde sie jetzt empfangen."And I certainly didn't know the German for "Tell them I will see them now". Somehow my brain was translating my spoken English words into German and making me hear German in English.

Moments later the manservant returned with Goebbels and Himmler. Goebbels was dressed in civilian clothes and carried a trilby hat in his hands; Himmler wore the dreaded black uniform of the SS. Both of them halted immediately on entering the room, clicked their heels together smartly and raised outstretched right arms in the German salute. "Heil Hitler."

After only the briefest pause I returned the salute in the time-honoured manner and with all the passion I could muster. For just a second I'd thought not to return their stupid salute, but thought better of it; it might give them reason to suspect things weren't all they should be. "Heil Hitler," I barked, with an impressively loud click of the heels of my boots.

We stood looking at each other, my visitors obviously waiting for me to take the lead. I stirred myself into motion, made for the desk and indicated the chairs by the wall. "Please, gentlemen, be seated." It came out in German again, as I now half-expected it would. I moved behind the large desk - sitting down I saw that the framed photograph I'd noticed earlier was of Eva Braun - and Goebbels and Himmler drew up chairs. Again they waited for me to speak first. Goebbels coughed, as if to prompt me.

"Remind me why you are here, gentlemen," I said. Artfulness was never my strongest point but the words seemed to come to me easily. Maybe the Devil had left a bit of Hitler in me, along with the Norman Smith?

"The concentration camp position, mein Fuehrer," said Himmler.

Concentration camp position? What did he mean? What *was* the concentration camp position? I searched my memory. Germany had been building concentration camps since March 1933, Dachau. But this was 1936. Whatever it was Goebbels saved me from further conjecture.

"And our need to step up the building programme of these very necessary facilities."

I eyed them coolly and replied immediately and firmly. "We will not be building any more concentration camps. On the contrary we will be tearing down all the concentration camps and setting free all the people who have wrongfully been incarcerated in them. And we will be doing it immediately. Immediately! Is that clearly understood?" At least that's what I meant to say. The words that came out of my mouth were "Oh you've no need to bother me with such trivialities, build as many as you wish, the more the merrier."

CHAPTER TWENTY TWO

Nuremberg, September 14, 1936.

"Russia planned a world revolution and German workmen would be used as cannon-fodder for bolshevist imperialism. But we Nationalist Socialists do not wish that our military resources should be employed to impose by force on other peoples what those peoples themselves do not want. Our army does not swear an oath that it will with bloodshed extend the National Socialist idea over other peoples, but that it will with its own blood defend the Nationalist Socialist idea and thereby the German Reich, it's security and freedom, from the aggression of other peoples...."

I raised my voice with each of the final words of this sentence so by the time I got to *'other peoples'* it was little more than a scream. I could feel my eyes bulging as I repeated the final two words and brought the heel of my hand down hard on the rostrum to further emphasise the point. Each and every one of the crowd of well over a hundred thousand gathered that day in the Nazi Party rally grounds at Luitpoldhain roared their approval. Cries of "Heil Hitler, Heil Hitler!" rang out and echoed off the surrounding buildings. As I mopped my brow with the back of my hand before I continued I could feel the veins standing out on my temples. The crowd was getting a real show from me today.

"The German people as soldiers is one of the best peoples in the world: it would have become a veritable 'Fight to the Death Brigade' for the bloody purpose of these international

disseminators of strife. We have removed this danger, through the National Socialist Revolution, from our own people and from other peoples...."

And so Hitler's rant, my rant, went on, whipping the crowd up into a such a frenzy of hate and loathing for anything or anyone not German, not Aryan, that long before my speech ended some half-an- hour and five thousand words later later they would have torn limb from limb anyone who dared get in the way of the advance of the National Socialist Party and its glorious leader.

I hadn't intended to arouse their passions with an attack on bolshevism of course. I hadn't wanted to inflame them by telling them that democracy was the canal through which bolshevism let's its poisons flow. I'd wanted to tell them to return home to their wives and children and live peacefully and peaceably and forget all about waging war on other countries to the greater glory of the mad little bastard now stood before ranting and raving and telling them to do exactly the opposite. In fact that's what I'd urged them to do. "Go home, put the kettle on, have a cup of tea, calm down, then take the wife and kids and the dog out for a walk, feed the ducks in the park maybe" I'd said. But as with my first day back on earth and on every occasion since, what I said and what came out of my mouth were two different things.

Is it possible for anyone to imagine how I felt? A man who hated Hitler, hated all he stood for, trapped in Hitler's body, and not only trapped in his body but behaving exactly as Hitler had behaved? Sanctioning torture, rubber-stamping mayhem, ordering murder, signing death warrants with the casual air of someone signing for a parcel delivered by the postman. If I thought I'd reached the depths of despair in having sex with a goat I was soon persuaded otherwise. If a goatherd had pitched up on my doorstep with a whole herd of goats I would gladly have had sex with every one of them rather than endure another second of what I was going through. The only good thing about being Hitler was that I no longer had a colostomy bag. I would have endured half-a-dozen colostomy bags and throw in a daily enema. The only thing I had to look forward to was my death in the Reich Chancellery bunker in Berlin in 1945. But then what? Where would I go then? Back to hell. For what other possible destination could there be for an evil despot responsible for the deaths of millions. What a prospect. What a bloody state to be in.

CHAPTER TWENTY THREE

The exorcist was dressed in a surplus and a purple stole. He opened his mouth and said, *"All-powerful God, pardon all the sins of your unworthy servant. Give me constant faith and power so that, armed with the power of Your holy strength, I can attack this cruel evil spirit in confidence and security."* While chanting these words, he sprinkled me with holy water.

*

It was quite by chance that I came up with the idea of getting a priest to try to exorcise the Devil from my body. Himmler and his sidekick Heydrich were constantly coming up with minority groups, sects, organisations, whatever - any band of people who didn't fit into the Nazi ideal - to add to the list of perfectly innocent human beings they had already discriminated against, the majority of whom were now either in concentration camps or had only escaped them by fleeing the country in fear of their lives. I knew from my scholarship of the events leading up to the war that Hitler had more or less given the Gestapo bosses *carte blanche* to single out for persecution anyone they wished. Heydrich in particular seemed to take immense pleasure in his work. And I of course went along with his choices. I always objected strongly, even after I'd been in Hitler's body for three months, even though I knew I'd be wasting my time, for the words that came out of my mouth were always words that sanctioned his choices, "Oh, that's a good idea," "Well *done* Heydrich I hadn't thought of that one," "Yes, do that, about time the buggers were taught a lesson." The only time I said "Well done Heydrich I hadn't thought of that one" and meant it was when he'd suggested Jehovah's Witnesses.

"Exorcists," he said, on this occasion, with a satisfied smile on his piggy-eyed wedge of a face.

I raised an eyebrow. "Exorcists?"

"Priests, religious maniacs who claim they can remove Satan from those who have been possessed by him."

I glared at him. "I know what exorcists are, dumbkopf. I was doubting the wisdom of consigning them to a concentration camp. Personally I would have thought that a German with the Devil removed from him is a purer human being than a German with the Devil inside...." I suddenly stopped, struck speechless at the wonderful possibility underlying my words.

Heydrich waited patiently for me to continue. When he realised I wasn't going to he said, "You are right of course, mein Fuehrer. As always."

My mind was working overtime. "I don't suppose you have by any chance already rounded up some of these exorcists?" My question was disingenuous, I already knew the answer; I was well aware of the way Heydrich worked - do things first and ask permission afterwards.

"Only a hundred or so as yet," he said, treating me to one of his oily smiles. "My apologies, mein Fuehrer. I should of course have realised that exorcists are extremely useful members of the German race. I will have them all released immediately."

"No!"

"You don't want me to release them?"

"Bring them to me."

"To you?"

"To me."

"All of them?"

"All of them."

Heydrich hesitated, intrigued. "Can I ask why?"

I searched my mind to come up with a good reason why I would want a hundred exorcists brought to my rooms in the Reichspalace. Then I realised I didn't need a reason. I had forgotten who I was. Hitler.

"No you cannot ask why," I snapped. "Now fuck off out of it and do as you're told."

*

Father Werner moved closer to me, made the sign of the cross and laid his palm on my forehead. I lay perfectly still while he recited the prayers of the exorcism ritual. He appealed to Christ, the Virgin Mary and the saints to aid him in the endeavour to save my soul. I had been warned by Father Werner to remain silent throughout. I had done so. The one hundred and eight other exorcists that Heydrich had delivered to me looked on, to a man willing the Devil to depart my body. I had given myself every chance.

Father Werner spoke. "*I exorcise you, Most Unclean Spirit! All Spirits! Every one of you! In the name of Our Lord Jesus Christ: Be uprooted and expelled from this Creature of God....*"

The rest of the exorcists joined in with him.

"*Let the love of Jesus drive your evil presence the body of this unfortunate so that he may be pure in spirit once again.*"

*

It was June 13, 1938. I had been Hitler for almost two years. A terrible, mortifying, two years. During that time I had witnessed wholesale acts of violence, presided over the worst atrocities of the Gestapo, overseen the building up of

205

the three main branches of the *Wehrmacht* and the civilian munitions industry that would arm them, and put in position plans to invade Europe and Russia. And there was not a thing I could do to stop myself.

There had been no respite. I could not even find comfort in the arms of Eva Braun. Hitler may have liked her, loved her indeed, if such a man was capable of love; Eva was a very attractive woman, prettier in the flesh than in the photographs I'd seen of her, with a lissom body and a demure air about her. A German Rose in fact. But not an English Rose. Not Kristin. I tried to make love to her once, just once, not because I wanted sex with her but in an attempt to take my mind of my terrible burden. The attempt failed totally. I couldn't get hard. She didn't seem at all surprised by this, accepted it as though it were a regular occurrence. (I recalled that I had once read that Hitler may have been impotent. All I can say is that the Norman Smith inside Hitler's body wasn't impotent; just the thought of Kristin and our time together, a frequent thought, was enough to give me an erection up to my throat.)

I was rarely alone. If I sought respite in my study in the Berghof or one of my offices in Berlin or Munich it was never long before there would be a knock on the door - Goebbels with some new ideas on propaganda he wanted to discuss, the vain and incompetent Goering forever demanding more funds for his beloved *Luftwaffe* , countless others with plans for this, that and the other, the list and the entreaties to add to it was endless.

It made no odds. On the rare occasion I was left to my own devices I had no devices to be left to. I was Norman Smith inside, not Hitler. I wanted to watch Manchester United, not Bayern Munich. I wanted to see a Robert de Niro or Jack Nicholson movie at the cinema not a Nazi propaganda film. When I went out for a meal I wanted steak and chips not dumplings and sauerkraut.

Not to be.

*

Father Werner made the sign of the cross and told me he would bring the exorcism to a conclusion. He placed a hand on my forehead, pressed a relic against his chest and said, "*Go away, Seducer! The desert is your home. The serpent is your dwelling. Be humiliated and cast down. For even though you have deceived men, you cannot make a mockery of God....He has prepared Hell for you and your angels.*" With that he lowered his arms and regarded me. The hundred and eight other exorcists looked on expectantly

Nothing happened. After a few moments the cleric said, "Do you feel nothing, my son?"

I shook my head. "Not a thing."

Father Werner sighed. "The Devil is deep within you. He has penetrated your very soul." He spread his hands in a gesture of defeat. "I have tried my utmost, mightily have I tried, but...."

And then it happened. A stirring, deep within my bowels. I can only describe the feeling as one of being really desperate for the lavatory, but much, much more than that. It felt as though I would literally burst. Five seconds later it was all over. Its genesis was a sudden sharp, stabbing pain in my anus, not up my anus but down through it. When the Devil entered my body it had felt like a red hot knife being plunged into my heart; now, when he departed it, he left it just as quickly, and with a great 'Whoosh', through my arse.

Very fitting, I remember thinking, just before my body became limp, thoroughly spent, and I lost consciousness.

CHAPTER TWENTY FOUR

I died on October 1 1980. A heart attack occasioned by a tram running me down in a Munich street. The Bauerstrasse, as I remember. The one newspaper that reported it - for by then my life had little interest for my fellow Germans - said that the multiple wounds I received to my chest and abdomen might have done for me anyway. Thankfully the heart attack saved me from a more painful death, for my demise was more or less immediate. One moment I was crossing the street to buy a newspaper - ironically the newspaper that reported my death - and the next moment I was dead.

Forty-two years had passed since the Devil had been driven from my body by the exorcists. The day after it happened I started putting plans into effect that would disband the German armed forces and the National Socialist Party. It proved to be an easier task than I had anticipated. There was little or no protest from the officers commanding the various arms of the *Wehrmacht*, still less from the men they commanded. They wished for war no more than did their counterparts in Russia and France and Great Britain. For the most part they were innocent souls, drawn into the situation, dragged screaming into it by their warmongering governments.

The disbanding and banishment of the Nazi Party met with more resistance. Goering was aghast at the idea. He thought I was mad and said so. I think I replied, "So what's new?" an expression both anachronistic and completely over

Goering's head, but true for all that. Himmler was beside himself at the thought of losing the SS, his dearly loved Gestapo along with it. Goebbels railed against it even more vociferously than his partners in crime. They were the three main opponents. There were others, von Ribbentrop and my deputy in the Nazi Party, Rudolf Hess, amongst them, but I was well aware that it was Goering, Goebbels and Himmler who were the main threat to my plans. I had them assassinated. Their seconds-in-command, automatically stepping into the shoes of their bosses, and no doubt surmising that a similar fate would befall them if they didn't toe the line, offered only token resistance. There was not so much as a peep out of von Ribbentrop and Hess.

I had no qualms about having the three murdered. It was the only way; they were all powerful men in their own right, quite influential enough to persuade others to have me assassinated had I not struck first. Initially, when I realised what I must do, I thought I might not be able to go through with it. But not for long; only until I remembered how many men, women and children they had already sent to an early grave, the hundreds of thousands who would follow them in the coming wars, the millions more who would perish in the concentration camps. After that it was an easy decision to make. I consoled myself, if I needed consoling, by reminding myself that I was only bringing their demise forward a few years; if things remained the same they would all die anyway, by their own hand before they could be executed for their war crimes.

The respective leaders of the armed forces argued for a slimmed-down peacekeeping presence. I told them that if there were no such things as armed forces there would be no such thing as war and therefore no need to keep the peace. It made perfect sense to me and enough sense to them to be persuaded to go along with it. There were still pockets of resistance but it only required me to remind the dissenters of the fate that had befallen Goebbels, Goering and Himmler and they soon forgot their arguments and came round to my way of thinking.

Within a month all the concentration camps had been emptied, their former inmates to hopefully be re-united with their loved ones. Their terrible accommodations of the past few years had been demolished; razed to the ground, bulldozed into the earth they had stood on. The *Wehrmacht* was no more. Auschwitz, along with its infamous gas ovens, was never built.

Three months later, just long enough for a coalition of the other main political parties in Germany to be formed into a government, I retired from public life. I was granted a generous pension by the new government, enough to live comfortably on for the rest of my life.

I began to live the rest of my life.

CHAPTER TWENTY FIVE

Although far from comfortably. This was Germany and I was an Englishman trapped in a German body. I couldn't settle. I didn't try very hard. On September 22, 1938 I moved to England. On September 27, 1938 I moved back to Germany. I couldn't speak English. I couldn't communicate. The Devil, although now out of me, had left me with a legacy, for, as was the case in Germany, I spoke in English but it came out in German. Everywhere I went people spat at me. Taunted me. Ragged me. There was no escape from it. I was struck several times; bloodied, knocked to the ground on more occasions than I care to remember.

Although war had been averted there were many people living in England, Jews in particular, who had fled from Germany and Poland and other European countries. The vast majority of them had been forced to leave their possessions behind. Many of them had lost husbands, wives, parents, children, in the concentration camps. And of course, even if I'd been able to speak English, I was highly recognisable as Hitler, the man who had been responsible for the loss of their loved ones. I pleaded with them. "Please, have mercy on me, I am Adolf Hitler, the man who averted the Second World War," but it came out as "Sei mir bitte gnaedig, Ich bin der Adolf Hitler, der Mann der den zweiten Weltkrieg verhindert hat." I don't know if any of them understood my words, probably some did, but the kindest reply I had was "Fuck off back to Germany you black-hearted twat."

In an effort to disguise myself, to give myself some sort

of chance, I bleached my hair blonde and shaved off my moustache. However no amount of tonsorial camouflage could stop me from speaking in German to the English, a race of people not renowned for their love of Germans since the First World War.

Back in Germany I settled in the small town of Neufahren, just outside Munich. And there I lived, uneventfully and on my own, for the rest of my days. No Eva Braun. She and I had soon drifted apart, not that we were ever 'together', and gone our separate ways; and I had no desire for any other woman to share my life. The one woman in the world I wanted hadn't even been born and I was quite unable to settle for anything less. I had tasted the finest truffled *fois gras*; I could not settle for potted meat or whatever its German equivalent was - probably potted pork.

On my return to Germany I let my hair grow back to its natural dark brown colour and re-grew my moustache. (Oddly, for some reason I couldn't fathom, I looked more ridiculous without the moustache than with it.) I had no ambition in life other than to grow as old as possible, even though the life I had was hardly filled with excitement; even though a life of poor quality it was better than what awaited me when I died. And which fiend would the Devil send me back as the next time I couldn't take another moment of his hell and sold my soul to him again? Saddam Hussein, Id Amin, Colonel Gadaffi? It didn't bear thinking about. I didn't think about it.

I determined to keep myself as fit as possible. I was then aged forty-nine, and reasonably healthy; my excesses had been in the form of subjugation, not eating and drinking, so I was still fairly fit and only a little overweight. I vowed to follow a healthy diet. Five a day would do the trick. Not to be. It might do the trick in the Great Britain I left in the year 2011 but this was Germany 1946. (Although the same situation still applies to this day if a trip I made to Cologne in 2009 is anything to go.) Getting five a day presented no problem at all. The trouble was that the five in question were five potatoes. Or five dumplings. Or five portions of pork in various guises. Or a combination of all three. Germans are very big on potatoes and dumpling and pork but very small on anything else. Oh and sauerkraut. They're big on that too. They don't seem to be able to look at a cabbage without pickling it.

Faced with a diet of potatoes, dumplings, pork and sauerkraut, hardly a recipe for a long life and odds on for a short one, I dispensed with the small lawn in my back garden and commenced to grow my own vegetables. I grew carrots, turnips, sprouts, onions, leeks, salad leaves, runner beans, and in a small greenhouse, tomatoes and peppers. I only grew cabbages once. When they had reached maturity they disappeared overnight, probably to be made into sauerkraut, so I didn't bother again. The produce I grew and ate helped me to live a long, if not very happy life.

I went back to England one more time, in 1972. For some reason, I don't know why, I began to wonder if there was another me, another Norman Smith, living in England. I couldn't see why there wouldn't be - the absence of a Second World War wouldn't have had any bearing on my being born, my father was too young to have been a soldier in it and possibly killed in action; and I knew for a fact that he had already met my mother in 1938 when they were both eight-year-olds. But I couldn't see why there would be. Norman Smith was in Germany, in Hitler's body but in Germany nevertheless, so it was impossible on the face of it.

But then I used to think it was impossible for there to be a heaven and a hell and I'd been to both of them and if that were possible anything was.

I had to find out.

*

It was around seven-o-clock in the evening when I arrived outside my old house in Harpurhey. Having got there I was at a loss as to what to do next. Knock on the door and say "Hello, is Norman in?" I couldn't very well do that. In any case it would come out in German and I wouldn't be understood. So I just stationed myself across the road and hoped for something to happen.

I saw my mother first. She came out of a house a few doors up the road, Mrs Scattergood's as I remember, they'd probably been gossiping, pulling the neighbours to bits. "Have you seen the colour of her curtains at Number 26?" She didn't pay me any attention, if indeed she saw me. I paid her little either, it wasn't my mother I'd come to see, I'd seen more than enough of her in life. About half-an-hour later my father came out through the front door. Probably going to the pub, it was a Monday, darts night. Another fifteen minutes went by. No sign of me at all. There was no one about so I crossed the road and chanced a look through the front window. My mother was watching TV. Coronation Street. Stan and Hilda Ogden arguing, Hilda doing most of the talking. I wasn't in the room, nor was there any trace of me, nothing I'd left lying around, no jigsaw puzzle I used to do on a baking board on the floor some evenings . I stepped back and gave it some thought. If there was a me, where would I be? It soon came to me; I wondered why it hadn't occurred to me before. Playing football. Nice evening like this, I'd be in the park playing togger with my mates, I was football mad.

I saw myself the moment I entered the park. Or at least I thought it was me. The boys, seven or eight of them, were about a hundred yards away. One of them was in short trousers. My mother wouldn't let me wear long trousers, like my mates, although I was the same age. Too expensive. "I didn't wear long trousers when I was twelve." "You were a girl, Mam." "Are you looking for a clout?"

I wanted to make sure it was me but I didn't want Norman to see me. There were some woods just behind where they were playing shooting in. I retraced my steps and approached the game through the woods. It was me all right, unmistakably, I was only twenty yards away. I watched for a short while from the cover of the trees. Suddenly one of the boys sliced the football and it headed straight for my hiding place. Norman, I, ran after it....

*

After, I returned to Germany and lived out the rest of my life. Then I died.

PART SIX

IM HIMMEL

CHAPTER TWENTY SIX

When I open my eyes I am not in hell, as I expect to be, but in heaven. I am seated on a bench, as was the case the first time I arrived in heaven, but it is not the bench in Piccadilly Gardens, Manchester; it is the bench in the park in Neufahren where I often used to sit reading my newspaper before taking a stroll by the lake where I would feed the ducks.

A man carrying a clipboard approaches. He stops, smiles, and says in German, "Allow me to introduce myself. I'm The Archangel Gunther, your mentor. I'll be...."

I butt in. "....meeting with me from time to time until I settle in. Yes, I know. I know all about heaven."

He is surprised. "You do?"

"I've been before. So if it's all the same to you I'll just get on with it."

*

Tentatively, my heart in my mouth, I lick my lips, take a deep breath and push gently on the door of the Hotel Königshof's Room 242. It eases open a few inches. I step inside. Kristin is in the room, waiting for me. She is just twenty years old. She is quite beautiful. No more beautiful than when I knew her as a fifty-year-old, just a more youthful beauty. We will very soon be making love. Although I am now aged ninety-one I am still capable of making love. I know that for sure; every week, once a week, until my death, to assure myself that I could still get an erection, I thought of Kristin and masturbated.

Why? Because without ever believing it was anything more than a pipe dream, without ever believing it was anything more than remotely possible, I have spent the last thirty-five years in the hope that I might be forgiven the terrible sins I perpetrated on the human race; that because I called a halt to them and saved the world from World War Two and the holocaust that when I died I just might be returned to heaven and not to hell. Along with the natural desire to keep out of the terrible place that is hell for as long as was humanly possible it was the reason I tried my hardest to keep healthy, to give myself the best chance of leading a long life - so that if and when I met up again with Kristin we would be lovers in every sense of the word. And now we will be.

I look at her and smile. My English Rose. She returns my smile. She says, "I think the moustache will have to go."

****

If you enjoyed reading I'm Heaven can you do me a favour? If you are a member of facebook, recommend it to your facebook friends, if you have a Twitter account, tweet your opinion of it, or if you have neither simply tell anyone in your email address book who you think might like it.

Thanks for this.

Terry Ravenscroft.

Also by Terry Ravenscroft

I'M IN HEAVEN

Amazon Customer review -
This is the best book I have read in years! The subject matter is dealt with in such a humorous manner but this is a real page turner! I have read all of Mr Ravenscroft's books and in my opinion this is THE BEST! Hilarious, sad, fascinating and a scintillating plot to boot! A must read! Very funny. - Martin K Davies

****

JAMES BLOND – STOCKPORT IS TOO MUCH

Amazon Customer review -
I'd come across Terry Ravenscroft quite recently via an author peer review site, and was delighted to discover how many amusing books he had written. This one lives up to the standard of the others I've seen, and keeps carefully just on the tasteful side of crude - I don't like crudity, sick humour or 'smut' but Terry somehow manages to avoid these things

while still dealing with the fundamentals of human existence. And James Blond's spoof credentials don't stop him from reminding us sometimes of the original, which highlights Ravenscroft's skill in humorous writing. There are even aliens! – Janey Fisher

****

CAPTAIN'S DAY

Amazon Customer review -
This is a very funny book. It will be enjoyed by golfers and non-golfers alike. In fact if Captains Day was like this in real life, lots more would take up the game. Refreshingly non pc with events that only the author could ever think of. Great fun and I doubt you have ever read anything like it before. – Cornishblue.

****

INFLATABLE HUGH

Amazon Customer review -
"Apparently your brother maintained the belief that having sex with an inflatable rubber woman was almost as beneficial in creating a feeling of well-being as the real thing. This being the case he viewed his operation more like a public service than a moneymaking operation. Which isn't to say he didn't make substantial profits from the sales ...."
Pugh's heart beat faster. Substantial profits. What a wonderful coming together of words.

With the above opening paragraph of Inflatable Hugh I was

219

*hooked. Terry Ravenscroft's tongue in cheek writing had me
laughing out loud from beginning to end. From the wily to
the ingenuous, from the morally indignant Vigilantes Against
Sex Toys to the crafty machinations of politicians, all are
depicted with subtle insight into character. In recommending
this as a 'great' read I could only paraphrase the author's
own writing: What a delightful coming together of words!* -
Rue.

****

FOOTBALL CRAZY

Amazon Customer review -
*Apart from being very very funny, Football Crazy is unique.
For me it's a marvellous mixture of Tom Sharpe and Ripping
Yarns with its larger-than-life characters that come alive in
your head as the story unfolds and the world of football
superstars meets the rich tycoon who's going to bring the
return of long-awaited success. Except we're talking Frogley
Town and a meat-pie millionaire. Oh - and Superintendent
Screwer who would see civil unrest in an impatient bus
queue. As is the way with the best caricatures, we've sort of
met the main characters before. We know elements of Donny
Donnelly, Joe Price and Superintendent Screwer do actually
exist in the real world; we can't quite place who and where
but we recognise them when we see them. I really do
recommend this book, it's a cracking story and, football fan
or not, it will bring a smile to your face. It's crying out to be
made into a one-off TV special.* - Anthony J McCrorie

****

DEAR AIR 2000

Amazon Customer review -
*I thoroughly enjoyed reading this book, couldn't put it down.
Mad-cap humour at its best. My only criticism is that it was
too short, I got through it in a day. Going off now to see
what else this guy has written that I might enjoy. Highly
recommended.* - ketch29

****

DEAR COCA-COLA

Amazon Customer review -
*Do not read this book whilst holding a cold drink, a hot
partner or anything squeezable. The genius of this man's
writing is a beautiful thing to read, dry, sharply observed
and above all cheap as chips on kindle downloads. As funny
as 'Dear Air 2000' but without the lasagne, although you
will never be able to look at Bisto gravy granules in quite the
same way ever again. Whatever you do download this and
help keep Terry Ravenscroft in Oxfam trousers and 2 bottles
of white wine.* – Lee Sylvester.

****

LES DAWSON'S CISSIE AND ADA

YouTube Reviews -
*"Were you virgo intacta?" "No just bed and breakfast." I'm
aching from laughing! Pure genius!*

*Was drinking a cup of tea when Ada said she was
approaching the change. When Cissie said "From which*

direction?" I lost it as I spat a mouthful of tea across the room. Classic, brilliant comedy.

****

Lightning Source UK Ltd.
Milton Keynes UK
UKOW051905240613

212751UK00001B/61/P